MW01146490

Cover art designed by
Cover photography b
Cover modeling by Nick Nesbitt

Copyright © 2013 by Nate Granzow

ISBN 10: 1490521712
ISBN 13: 978-1490521718

Note: This is a work of fiction. While the names of some public figures, locations, and actual world events are real, the characters in these pages and their exploits are entirely fictitious. Any resemblance to actual persons, living or dead, is entirely coincidental.

COGAR'S REVOLT

NATE GRANZOW

"Journalism is printing what someone else does not want printed: Everything else is public relations."

—George Orwell

NATE GRANZOW

1

A Fine How Do You Do

Cairo, Egypt, January 2011

The rear windshield exploded, a wave of fragmented glass shards crashing against the back of my neck as rifle rounds tore through the taxi's interior.

"Jesus fucking Christ, lose them quick or we're dead!" I screamed, pushing my palm harder against the sucking chest wound of the unconscious man in the car's passenger seat. Daring a glance over my shoulder, I spotted a black SUV trailing closely behind our vehicle as we weaved through the crowded streets of downtown Cairo. Illuminated by the passing streetlights as he hung from the vehicle's open passenger window, a balding, one-eyed brute I knew only as Kek shuffled a fresh magazine into his AKS-74.

The Syrian mercenary worked on behalf of the Muslim Brotherhood—one of Egypt's leading political factions at the forefront of the civil unrest that had brought me here. But they would never openly acknowledge his allegiance to their cause. Kek brought with him a reputation for creating violent chaos—the kind I was suddenly experiencing firsthand. But he was uncontrollable: one of those spasmodic variables that gets turned loose on an enemy in the faint hopes he doesn't double-back and kill his handlers. Collateral damage was a meaningless phrase to this sociopath. Anything or anyone who happened to end up between him and his target—me, in this case—had to be destroyed without mercy. That was his credo, his doctrine: Once he'd set his sights on killing you, he would continue tirelessly until the job was done.

I couldn't tell if the scarred-over shrapnel wound spanning the width of the mercenary's cheek had pulled his lips up in a grimace, or if the bastard was smiling as he pinned the rifle's folding metal stock against his shoulder and sighted the weapon on my head.

For those who don't know me very well, you may wonder how a reasonably intelligent American journalist—one with enough experience to know better— manages to get himself hunted like a convict in one of the most volatile cities in the world.

That's an excellent question.

2

Friday of Anger

"Ladies and gentlemen, we are now on our final approach to Cairo International Airport. Please return your trays and seat backs to their full, upright, and locked position."

An elbow slammed into my ribcage, jarring me from the drunken half-sleep I'd been in for the past few hours. Bleary-eyed, I looked over at the man who'd woken me.

"We're here," he said bluntly.

"Thanks for the gentle wake-up, Perry."

Perry Rothko, my archenemy in the journalism world, pulled a pearl-handled comb from his pocket and carefully swept over his already neatly kept blond hair. I brushed the pile of empty miniature vodka bottles from my tray and locked it in place; then began smoothing the wrinkles out of my suit jacket, looking at my rival more closely as the sleep cleared from my vision. Had he shaved during the flight? Scratching my cheek, I felt the sandpaper stubble that I should have dealt with two days ago. And I didn't need to look at a mirror to know my hair was a riotous mess—nothing like the conditioned artwork of my adversary.

The two of us had been seated next to each other on this flight purely through piss-poor luck. I always tried my damnedest to avoid the man, but we were regularly sent on similar assignments—generally into the same disfigured, war- and famine-plagued cities around the world. Perry represented the *New York Times* while I freelanced on behalf of the *Chicago Herald*, on retainer as their no-fucking-way-anyone-else-on-staff-is-gonna-do-it war correspondent. Though this probably seems like a trivial distinction, you have to understand that much of my hostility toward Perry stems from the fact that his position at his publication was originally meant for me.

Seven years before, when Perry and I both worked for the *Herald*, we traveled as a team to cover the war in the Darfur region of Sudan. It was Perry's first big opportunity to get out of the country—a sort of trial run in the field—and my editor, Kailas Raahi, sent me along to ensure he didn't screw it up.

Though initially friendly, it took me about five minutes after our introduction to pick up on Perry's subtle, but nonetheless palpable, Machiavellian nature. The man simply oozed charm and, admittedly, had the looks to back it up. He put that charm to hard use, seducing every woman at the office in turn. I later learned that he'd said more than a few unsavory things about my character to these women and other members of the staff—a juvenile attempt to ensure I wouldn't pose any competitive threat to his future womanizing.

This proved two things to me: first, that he'd say or do just about anything for the fleeting attention of a beautiful girl—a dangerous character flaw that can get some vital parts of a male's anatomy forcibly removed in some parts of the globe. Second, that I couldn't depend on him to have my back in the inevitably demanding assignment we were about to embark on.

Now, I've never pretended to be a shining light of morality, and I can forgive a great many flaws in my fellow man. Perry was clearly a conniving prick, but I thought maybe that competitive attitude of his would make him an asset in the field.

Upon our arrival in the Sudan, I learned that Perry had even less common sense than he had principles—an inexcusable flaw that endangered both of us. Within hours of our arrival, Perry began walking through the streets loudly asking merchants and ranchers if they knew where we could find some rebels to interview.

When that didn't work, he figured he'd grease the wheels a little, and began waving a wad of cash in front of their noses in hopes of getting a response. That was the point at which we parted ways. My intuition proved to be advantageous, because I produced what I still consider the finest article in my career shortly thereafter. My source, an officer in the Sudanese Liberation Movement, provided me with indisputable evidence—photos, video, and reports—that the government-backed militia forces responsible for the civilian massacres in the region were receiving training from Islamic Jihadists with ties to Al-Qaeda. It was good stuff. Not good for the people of Sudan, obviously, but powerful and timely information for the readers back home.

As I waited at my hotel for a flight out of the country—feeling unusually smug and pleased with myself for a job well done—Perry came limping through the door. Though dirty and beaten, he had somehow survived his idiocy and managed to make it to the safety of the hotel bar. I still kick myself for not seeing through his conspicuously magnanimous offer to buy me a drink. Stunned that the fool was still in one piece, I reluctantly accepted. I made it halfway through my glass of scotch before the lights went out. When I came to, my article was gone, and so was Perry. He had stolen my work, and it was that article—*my article*—that landed him his job at the *Times*. To this day I can't stand the smell of scotch.

Surely, if it hadn't been for that one lucky—nay, criminally wrought—break, Perry would have fallen into obscurity or, more likely, gone to work writing copy for pharmaceutical advertisements.

Contact your doctor immediately if bleeding from the eyes or ears occurs.

In terms of raw talent, the guy was a woefully mediocre writer and a worse researcher. When it came to honesty and integrity, he was utterly bankrupt.

I slid open the window blind and stared out over the aircraft's wing. Thousands of tan buildings, partially obscured by heavy smog and strung together in tight clusters, gave the earth the texture of a blotchy scab. As we neared the ground, the buildings took on more definitive shape, evoking images of some post-apocalyptic dystopia where the few survivors huddle indoors as dust storms sweep through empty streets. From here, even the greenery looked brown.

"Where are you staying, Cogar?" Perry asked. It was his first attempt at small talk since we'd left Seoul nine hours ago, and his tone betrayed that he didn't care what my answer would be.

"I don't know yet." *But considering how tight Kailas keeps the budget, probably a French youth hostel.*

"Yourself?"

"The Fairmont," he said, unbuttoning his shirt cuff and folding his sleeve back neatly.

"Nice." That narcissistic jackass would be sleeping in silk sheets and ordering room service while I shared a room with a dozen unwashed adolescent world travelers, fighting off coordinated waves of flea attacks and sleeping on a cot beneath an itchy wool army blanket.

"I guess so. I'm just tired of being ordered into countries where toothpaste and toilet paper are luxuries. I probably spend more on my medical-evac and kidnapping, rescue, and extortion insurance than I do my retirement savings, you know?"

I didn't blink. Only Perry, a man who had been traveling the world for the last decade, seeing the most forlorn and the most exquisite places on the planet, living the life of the ultimate adventurer, could still sound like a juvenile sorority sister on spring break. No one ever believed me when I'd tell them about Perry and the privileged, idiotic, discriminatory things he only seemed to say around me. Everyone who'd met him thought nothing but the best of his character.

"Hey, I meant to ask you, did you end up hooking up with that Australian chick back in Seoul? She never returned my call. I figured she must have fallen victim to the charms of the infamous Grant Cogar." He laughed earnestly and elbowed my arm, knocking it off the rest separating us and into my thigh. The question, though posed as nothing more than manly chatter, was probing—his ego couldn't handle not knowing if I'd won over a woman he'd tried for.

"I'm flattered, but you think I could have scored with a woman of that caliber?" I said with a smile, remembering the graceful curves of Jessica's hips and how she'd felt against my skin when we'd made love.

"Fair point. She was well out of your league."

Out of my league? I was being sarcastic, dickhead.

Perry continued airily, "But hey, a guy can dream. I once had a yoga instructor that was along those same lines, you know? Just an absolute goddess. The kind where you think, 'they don't make men good-looking enough for a woman like her'. Young, athletic, flexible…anyway, halfway through showing me the proper posture for a downward dog position…."

"Perry, I get it. I'm sure it was great."

"It was. Hey, with any luck, this whole rebellion thing will work itself out in a couple days, and we'll be able to get some time in with the native girls," he said, reaching up and turning off the overhead fan as the plane's wheels chirped against the tarmac.

Sure, Perry. Because Egypt has such a progressive outlook on extramarital sex, right? I imagined him tethered spread-eagle in a town square, a crowd of village elders sharpening their blood-pocked scissors in preparation for his neutering. I'm surprised it hasn't happened already.

As the plane taxied to the gate, I followed Perry into the aisle, slinging my venerable leather duffel bag onto my shoulder as we disembarked the plane. I was too tired to even unzip his bags as they swung in front of me on the way out. Reaching the gate, I gave Perry a two-fingered wave without looking at him and headed for the exit.

"See you," he said, as he made for the baggage claim. He always packs several suitcases too many—too many for a man who should have learned better by now, anyway. Luggage slows a reporter down, makes him a target to thieves, and only marginally improves comfort in the field. He probably spends more time waiting on lost luggage than doing his job.

I ran my hand through my hair and yawned— recoiling at the smell of my own breath and the cumulative odor from every other passenger on the plane embedded in my clothing. My head ached, and I knew I'd need alcohol, coffee, or sleep in the near future in order to avoid becoming a very unpleasant person. I trudged toward the exit.

The truth was, I didn't really want this assignment. It would have been nice to spend another few weeks in Seoul, drinking, making love by the hour to that Australian beauty Perry mentioned—she was crazy about me, by the way—and thinking nothing of work. But if I'd put off traveling to Cairo for even a few more days, the job would have become much harder. Wars and tumultuous political changes happen fast and fluidly in their first weeks of existence. Then, they inevitably bog down as momentum grinds to a halt, new players emerge, and plans go awry. Show up to the party late, and you'll spend more time and money getting less information, and may even find it difficult to get into the conflict zone at all without spending obscene sums of cash on a "fixer"—one of those swarthy locals with contacts in the government or criminal underworld that can help you get where you need to go. I didn't have the cash for that. Freelance reporters like myself are cheap whores paid for their services with only thin, slatternly wads of cash and a look of contempt. Moreover, hiring a fixer doesn't guarantee that you'll actually find the right people to talk to or arrive at your intended destination in one piece. Many times, your new friend finds it more appealing to first accept payment for their services, and then facilitate your kidnapping.

When a conflict's momentum stalls out, but journalists from around the world continue trickling in to cover it, demand for goods and services goes way up and the market thrives. Thirsty? You're going to pay handsomely for that bottled water. Need a ride to the embassy? The driver won't even turn the key without danger pay, plus interest, plus gas money for his troubles. Not that I didn't want to help Hakim make more money than he'd seen in a decade by hiring him as a guide, but if I could find a way around it and still get my story? Yeah, I'll take the earlier flight.

After a quick glance around, I spotted an espresso machine at the terminal's entrance and fumbled in my pocket for money. Withdrawing the little bit I had, I thumbed the paper, staring with dismay at the likeness of mustached men bedecked in traditional Korean garb on each bill. I'd have to find a currency converter just to get a goddamn cup of joe. I stuffed the bills back into my pocket, resolving to hail a taxi and make a beeline for the bar of the most expensive hotel in town, posthaste. That was my foolproof custom when visiting countries where I had no existing connections. There, I'd find journalists, photogs, and expats I could pump for information and leads.

And get a drink.

Okay, mostly to get a drink.

"It looks as though you're out of luck."

Over my shoulder, a trio of Egyptian men approached.

"It's not about luck—it's just shitty planning. Can I help you?" I asked, my fingers plastered longingly to the coffeemaker's glass front.

"Perhaps. What is your name?" asked the one in the center, looking down at a printed sheet of paper in his hand.

Suddenly noting the man's khaki uniform and the two burly, beret-wearing soldiers standing at both his shoulders, I responded, "Doctor Cogar, to whom do I owe the pleasure?" I extended my open hand.

"You are no doctor, Mr. Cogar," he said, shaking it firmly.

"Well, strictly speaking, I'm a veterinarian. But I've got eight years of school loans to prove I've earned the title 'doctor'," I chuckled weakly.

"You are no veterinarian, either," he replied, holding up the paper in his hand. "You are Grant Cogar, war correspondent. Approximately 180 centimeters tall; weight—80 kilograms," he said, eyeing me. "I'm sorry to say, Mr. Cogar, but you haven't aged well."

"Let me see that," I said sorely, tugging the paper from his fingers. On it, a familiar-looking young man with short, golden brown hair, blue eyes, and an arrogant smirk looked back at me. The photo had been taken early in my career, and I immediately noticed an absence of scars, bags under my eyes, and my usual three-day beard.

"My name is Colonel Saif al-Orabi of the *Jihaz Amn ad-Daoula*—the State Security Investigations Service." Offering me a handshake, he continued, "I admire your creativity, but I cannot think that anyone has ever believed such a ridiculous façade."

The colonel appeared to have once been a handsome man, but his visage reflected his age: His aquiline nose had clearly been broken at some point in the distant past, his hairline had receded to the tops of his ears, and his eyes, lined with dark circles, reflected an exhaustion brought on by decades spent in a stressful career. But despite his worn appearance, his six-foot-tall frame stood straight with a rigid deportment characteristic of a lifelong military man.

I shrugged. "Say anything with enough conviction and people will believe it. If you can't impress them with your intellect, baffle them with your bullshit." I handed back my dossier.

Bursting forth with a sudden laugh loud enough to warrant startled looks from those standing nearby, the colonel said, "I like that a great deal, Mr. Cogar. I'll remember that."

Of course, there's also that bit about bullshit walking.

Clearing his throat and looking around him uncomfortably, the colonel said, "Mr. Cogar, I'd like to invite you to my humble home for dinner tonight, if you'd be so kind as to join me and a few of your associates." He gestured toward where Perry stood waiting at the wrong baggage carousel, trying—unsuccessfully from the looks of it—to send a text message on his phone. "Consider it a welcome to the country."

Rubbing the stubble on my cheek, I looked from the colonel to his men. A healthy dose of skepticism can be life saving when visiting a new, almost-always hostile, place. This colonel could very well be an impersonator—part of some extremist group looking to capture and hold ransom a gullible American journalist. Even if he was the legitimate article, there was no way for me to be certain that he had my best interests in mind. I still wasn't up to speed on the situation here, and I'd feel eternally foolish if I were to volunteer for capture only to be deported or executed. "I'd love to, but…."

"Mr. Cogar," the colonel's tone suddenly changed to barely-restrained hostility, the two soldiers beside him taking an aggressive step forward, hands reaching for the exposed pistol grips protruding from their nylon drop-leg holsters. "I would be offended if you didn't accept."

3

Path of Least Resistance

I jostled uncomfortably in my seat as Perry and I rode through the streets of Cairo in the back of Colonel Orabi's private car, a glossy black Cadillac with dark, tinted windows. We moved slowly, traffic gridlocked and the blare of horns constant. *Tok toks*, sputtering two-stroke, three-wheeled auto rickshaws, zoomed between cars and buses at 60 miles-per-hour, zigzagging their way through the congestion with their passengers clinging to the vehicle's frame, praying for safe delivery. Minibuses, stuffed with twice their capacity in turbaned men on their way to work, rolled recklessly by, piloted by drivers with little consideration for the safety of their passengers or the public. Cairo had outgrown herself; the city's roads, never meant to accommodate two million cars, received no reprieve from sunup to sundown, its inhabitants making do with what they had even when it meant spending most of their waking hours in gridlocked traffic.

Snap. Perry looked out his window blankly, chewing and popping bubbles in a piece of mint gum. The scent of his cologne blended agreeably with that of the cigarette smoke embedded in the vehicle's upholstery.

He's far too clean to be a reporter.

Snap. Moving my hand until it hovered just behind his head, I waited for him to try his luck once more.

"So Mr. Cogar, I've done a little research on your exploits," the colonel said from the passenger seat. "You're quite the prolific writer."

Grudgingly moving my hand back into my lap, I replied, "I've been at this for a while."

"I particularly enjoyed your work in Jerusalem during the Second Lebanon War. As I'm sure you know, Israel and Egypt have not enjoyed the most amiable of relationships."

The mosquito-like drone of a passing motorcyclist was suddenly punctuated by a loud *thump* as something impacted the hood of the Cadillac. Looking over the driver's shoulder, I watched as a brick tumbled across the polished surface, leaving a deep triangular indentation trailed by a series of deep scratches. Our driver had his pistol drawn and out the window before the projectile skidded off the car and to the pavement, but the vandal had already motored out of range.

"Friend of yours?" I asked.

"That's a real shame," Perry said, craning his neck to see the damage. "That really did a number on the paint."

The colonel worked his jaw angrily, nodding to the driver, gesturing for him to holster his weapon. Orabi abruptly withdrew a pack of Marlboros and offered them to us over his shoulder.

Perry declined. "Thanks, but I don't smoke. Stains the teeth, and it's hard on the respiratory system, you know? I'm something of a runner. Recreationally."

Orabi raised his eyebrows, but didn't reply. Turning to me, he made the same offer.

"Coffee first, if you don't mind, Colonel."

He shrugged, slipping a smoke into his mouth. "In regards to your article, Mr. Cogar, I never felt the heat beneath my collar as I typically do when reading news stories written by Americans on the subject," he mumbled as he stared at the lesion in his car's hood, obviously still preoccupied with the damage to his vehicle.

"Why do you say that?"

"It seems to me that, unlike your compatriots, you don't let ego or personal bias influence your writing. I never felt as though you were trying to sway my opinion with your work." The cigarette seemed to calm him, his voice becoming lower and more relaxed as twin streams of smoke rolled out his nostrils. Colonel Orabi struck me as the type who never enjoyed a moment of true rest, even the hours spent sleeping or eating viewed only as distractions necessary to survival. That, I had no doubt, was just a side effect of the real essence of his character— that of an anal-retentive control freak. One of those people who demanded every detail fall into place, even if it came at the cost of lost hair and premature aging. He would have that dent buffed out before morning.

"That's very flattering, Colonel. I do my best, but I'd be lying if I said that I'm capable of staying completely indifferent. Words are as much a reflection of the writer as the subject."

Hearing the colonel's commendation of my work filled me with no small sense of pride. Though I'll be the first to admit that I'm fit to be no one's role model, and have embraced more than a few habits and vices that have put me out of the running for sainthood, one thing has always been sacred to me, and will be until the day I die: integrity in my writing. Journalism doesn't need any help being perceived as the preferred career of liars and perjurers, requiring the same absence of moral fortitude typical of lawyers and politicians.

"Your self-awareness is, at least, worthy of respect," the colonel replied.

Perry tapped Orabi on the shoulder. "No doubt you've read some of my work. I was there during the Second Lebanon War, too. Made the front page of the *Times*—'Hezbollah raids Israel'."

"Yes, I seem to remember that one clearly," the colonel sighed as he reached for the radio's volume knob and turned it up.

Crossing a leg over my knee, I smiled and sat back in my seat. I was beginning to like this guy.

For the next half hour, we listened to President Mubarak give a speech as we passed by the city's towering apartment complexes, hotels, and mosques, each an analogous shade of tan. The city felt swollen, bloated and ready to burst. Nowhere could a foot of free space be found. It reminded me of the Brazilian *favelas*—squatter settlements with ragtag buildings constructed so close to one another you could run a quarter mile jumping from rooftop to rooftop.

"What's he saying?" I asked the colonel as loud, assumedly fake clapping interrupted the voice on the radio.

"He's pledging to form a new government."

"With him staying on as president, right? I don't suppose that's what the people are looking for."

"No, they want him to step down. There will be more protests tonight, I'm sure." He drew deeply at his cigarette as his foot beat an irregular rhythm on the floorboard.

I paused before continuing my inquiry and looked at Perry. Though outwardly fixated on the passing scenery, I knew him to be just conniving enough to actually be listening intently to our conversation with aims to use my questions and the colonel's answers to write his own article. I didn't want to help him in any way, but I didn't want to waste an opportunity to question someone with so much insight into the political and military scene, either. After brief contemplation, I decided to proceed. After all, even if I were to give Perry every quotation I had and a thorough outline of how I'd write the article, he'd still find a way to mess it up.

"Colonel, tell me honestly, how bad are things here?"

"Do you mean in terms of the rioting?"

"That seems like a good place to start."

"Looting has become rampant. Prisons have been burned down and inmates scattered to the wind, and just before I found you, the police were withdrawn from the streets and our soldiers brought in."

"Is that why you asked us to join you?"

"This is an effort to keep you and Mr. Rothko safe."

"How considerate."

The car slowed before a set of wrought-iron gates, which swung open automatically to reveal a paved driveway leading to a grand two-story building, its pearl-colored walls illuminated by garden lights hidden among the bushes. An armored Mercedes-Benz SUV sat parked near the entrance, a squad of soldiers encircling it as they smoked cigarettes, their rifles resting in the crooks of their arms.

"You've got some tough-looking gardeners on staff, Colonel," I said as one of the soldiers slipped the cigarette from his mouth, spat, and stared at me defiantly.

Laughing, Orabi said, "Just a safeguard for tonight. With things as chaotic as they've been, I'd rather not take any chances on security." As we came to a stop, he said, "Welcome to my home, gentlemen. I believe we are the last ones to arrive."

Small groups of men and women congregated near a broad staircase that swept gracefully toward the pillared entryway.

"Colonel, who all is attending this evening?" Perry asked, gesturing toward the crowd.

"Reporters like you," the colonel said as he stepped from the car and stretched his back. He waved to two men smoking cigars on the building's upper balcony. "Please feel free to leave your bags with my men, I'll have them delivered to your hotel."

The colonel's driver popped the trunk latch and reached for my bag without making eye contact.

"I've got it, actually. Thanks," I said hastily, slinging its strap over my shoulder.

"Are you sure, Mr. Cogar? It might be a bit inconvenient hauling that about all evening," the colonel said, tapping the bag lightly.

Swinging the duffel out of his reach, I replied, "I appreciate your concern, Colonel. But I'll be fine."

In the life of the traveling reporter, few things can be considered constant. You have no time and often no inclination to form lasting friendships or relationships, you sleep in a different bed (or no bed at all) each night, and possessions must often be limited to those things you can carry on your person. As childish as it may sound, that worn-out, frayed, dirty-ass bag was my traveling companion and comfort blanket.

I also don't like strangers—especially inquisitive government officials—rooting through my shit.

As we made our way inside, I recognized the faces of my competition. Names were always tough for me to remember, but their features were familiar enough for me to recall which publication they worked for and the dirty secrets they didn't know everyone already knew. *There's BBC guy with the kid who's a heroin-dealer, that unusually tall lady from USA Today who refuses to wear underwear, the chubby homophobic from the Washington Post, mustache from the Daily News with the sex-addict wife...*

I reached for my phone. I didn't know what the colonel was planning by having what seemed like every foreign journalist in the country brought to his home, but I was hoping Kailas would have some insight.

"I'm afraid neither the Internet nor your cell phone will work, Mr. Cogar," the colonel said, placing his hand gently on my wrist. "The protestors use these as tools to congregate. You're more than welcome to use my personal satellite phone to contact your family or your editor, though."

"I'd appreciate that."

Glancing back at the other reporters, I grinned. They were undoubtedly going crazy not being able to post regular updates to their Twitter followers back home. The modern reporter was no longer just a familiar byline readers recognized in the Sunday paper, but a self-designated celebrity. Remaining unbiased and largely anonymous to the public had fallen out of vogue; instead, those who made a habit of being self-aggrandizing and politically polarized were rewarded with book deals and their own segments on morning television. Maybe my refusal to stoop to that level is just my clinging to an outdated perception of how reporters are supposed to behave. I'd grown up trying to emulate the likes of Robert Capa, the WWII combat photojournalist who faced Nazi machine guns on Omaha beach, befriended brilliant men like John Steinbeck, and even had a fling with Ingrid Bergman—the Hollywood beauty who starred alongside Humphrey Bogart in *Casablanca*. And you know what? No one today knows who he was. He was too busy getting his story to care whether he was in fashion with the people back home or whether the next generation would remember his name. That's the kind of reporter I wanted to be: as free and easy as Hunter S. Thompson without the controversy. Besides, I couldn't give two evanescent fucks about what celebrities were up to from moment to moment, so why the hell would I try to become one? Unlike my fellow reporters, I was perfectly content doing my job, enjoying the occasional company of a beautiful woman, and throwing back a few shots too many when I'd finished a story.

"The phone's just up the hall on the right," the colonel said. I smiled at him graciously, though I knew the phone would almost certainly be bugged or monitored. Not that I cared.

I had nothing to hide.

Nothing they'd be interested in, anyway.

I made my way up the hallway, following Orabi's directions until I came upon a mahogany cabinet. It took me a moment to find the satellite phone he'd discreetly placed behind a small granite bust of the pharaoh Ramesses. Opening the phone stand's doors, I stuffed my bag inside like a squirrel burying a nut, grabbed the phone, and dialed Kailas' personal number. It was probably the middle of the night back in Chicago, but I fully intended to interrupt his sleep the way he had mine time and again when assigning me a story.

"Hello?"

"You sound mighty perky, what time is it there?"

"Noon. Why?"

Oops. Not even close.

"Oh, I just figured it was later—didn't want to interrupt your sleep."

"Didn't stop you from trying though, did it? You rude sonofabitch."

The Indian-American was a prickly bastard to most everyone, me included. But despite his tough exterior and unforgiving, usually crude demeanor, I liked Kailas. He'd been my mentor since high school, and though he'd deny it to the death if you asked him, I'm one of the few people he trusts. The obscenities and insults we level at one another are really a sign of fondness.

"So the situation is a little different than you'd led me to think when you sent me here, Kailas. Thanks for that."

"How so?"

"Well, I didn't even make it out of the airport before I was grabbed up by some colonel from the…dammit, what did he call it…State Security Investigations Service."

"So you've already been captured, and now you're calling me in hopes that I can get you to the embassy?"

"When have I ever called you asking for help?"

"Oh, let's see...Shanghai, Jerusalem, Haiti..."

"Okay, okay."

"...Darfur, Monrovia..."

"Yeah, but have I ever really *needed* your help?"

"True, somehow you keep finding a way back here. You're like a stray dog that way. And for some reason I keep offering you work. What's the definition of insanity? Doing the same thing over and over and expecting a different result?"

"You're not insane, you just know talent when you see it."

Swiping Ramesses from the tabletop, I slid the pad of my thumb over the Basset Hound-like ears of the statue's nemes headdress.

"Right. So were you the only one this colonel nabbed?"

"He's got everyone here, Kailas."

"Well that's good. It sounds like he's trying to keep tabs on you. Mubarak's public relations specialist with a gun."

"Yeah, that's what I figured. Great. Getting started under scrutiny; I'm going to end up in prison for sure."

I gave the bust a small squeeze. A soft cracking sound preceded the statue's head completely separating from the body at the neck; it landed dully atop the carpeted floor.

Oh goddamit.

"I don't doubt it. By the way, Cogar, before I forget: Some guy named Hasan keeps calling me saying you're late on your rent payment."

"Well, did you pay him?"

Making a noise as though I had punched him in the throat, Kailas replied, "Fuck no. Am I your mother? Your personal life is just that, Cogar. Personal."

"The reason I haven't paid him is due in large part to your sending me all over the planet following news stories for *your* publication. I haven't been home in a month. Send him a check and take it out of my pay."

I returned the statue to the table. Balancing the head atop the neck, I carefully aligned the seams of the crack.

Kailas grumbled, "You smug bastard. Making me your personal bitch accountant. I should have sent Logan to Cairo and had you take his place in Baghdad—that'd teach you to give me shit."

"Right, Kailas, the thought of getting sent back to Iraq, *again*, terrifies me. I cut my teeth in that sandbox, remember? But speaking of smug bastards, guess who accompanied me to Cairo?"

"I haven't the slightest idea, Cogar."

"Our old pal Perry Rothko."

"Jesus. You mean that sniveling excuse for a human being is still alive? I was certain someone would have shot or lynched that fucker back in Seoul."

Mirroring my feelings towards Perry, Kailas felt complicit in my adversary's ascent to the big time; had he just waited to run the story until he had spoken to me, he would have avoided getting played like I had. Perry had fooled everyone at the *Herald*, struck it lucky with the folks at the *New York Times*, and then split before any of us could so much as pick our jaws up off the floor.

"They nearly did, but the man's like a cockroach. Just when you thought you got rid of him, there he is again—back and bolder than before." Actually, he was worse than a cockroach. Though insects can't speak, I'd imagine if they could, they'd at least choose their words more carefully than Perry. My rival, like so many news reporters today, has never once been held accountable for his morally suspect, overtly biased, and in some cases, downright factually incorrect reporting.

"Cogar, hold on a second." In the background, I could hear Kailas shouting, 'your voice recorder not catching the interview isn't a fucking excuse for missing deadline. Call him back and do it again if you have to.' I held the phone between my shoulder and neck as Kailas railed against one of his reporters. It seemed appropriate background noise for trying to recollect Perry's most slipshod work.

South Ossetia.

Definitely South Ossetia.

Back in 2008, Perry and I were both sent to cover a short-lived series of battles in which Russian forces rolled into this beautiful area north of Armenia—covered in lush mountains and low pastureland—and beat the piss out of the invading Georgian military in just a few days. Perry wrote an article that insisted the Russians' large-scale offensive strike had been an unprovoked act of war and a brutish display of their military power on the world stage during the otherwise peaceful Olympic games in Beijing—not an unpopular view at the time. Most of the western papers had been quick to hop on this same accusatory bandwagon, largely because they're fucking lemmings and using critical thinking skills is hard work they have no intention of doing.

A little research into the events leading up to the war would have revealed Georgia's instigation of the conflict by its attempt to retake separatist South Ossetia by force, or more importantly, the fact that the entire region had been a tinderbox for decades. Both parties were, in some capacity or another, guilty of violent attacks and attempts to undermine their opposition. Russia had been prepared for war; Georgia just gave them an excuse to declare it. The entire ordeal, despite its brevity, was a quagmire for any reporter to summarize or draw conclusions from succinctly—too many factors dating back too many years. Large, goose-stepping uniformed armies going nose to nose at sunrise in the name of God and country just don't happen anymore. Instead, wars of today are comprised of any number of power struggles between scuffling warlords, clans, or political groups; no clear battle lines are drawn, and no real rules of engagement are followed. It can be hard telling the difference between a modern war and an Afghani family reunion.

Through the phone's speaker, Kailas's voice suddenly changed to one of false joviality. "Well goddamn. Maybe we should just run this piece with the headline *Legislator won't pick up the fucking phone*. Or here's a good one: *Reporter procrastinates, can't get needed quotes to meet deadline*."

Despite Perry's brave attempt to provide his employer with a story worthy of their readership, he managed to first mistakenly call the Georgian president— a man named Mikhail Saakashvili—Mikhail Gorbachev. Yep, ol' Gorby—the former head of state of the Soviet Union who would have been on the wrong side of the conflict had he not been out of politics for *20 years*. It's just a typo, right? That's an easy mistake to make, and the copyeditors at the *Times* should have caught it. But then Perry proceeded to disparage the Russian government using completely fictional casualty numbers to fit his story, skewing them to look as though the Russians were suffering extreme losses and dealing enormous collateral damage to the civilian population. His article read like a piece of Georgian propaganda. The most amateur, wet-behind-the-ears journalist knows better than to report with such obvious bias. But writing concise, honest, dispassionate articles takes hard work and endless hours of interviews, research, and front-line exposure. Perry's reporting process, conversely, is like water: He can always be counted on to take the path of least resistance. It was just easier for him to fictionalize the conflict than to report it accurately.

Most readers never noticed.

Misinformation is a disease and Perry Rothko is one of the most promiscuous carriers there is. Back at my apartment in Chicago, I have an entire desk drawer devoted to the multitudinous cutouts of Perry's errors made throughout his career and the subsequent half-hearted corrections issued. The one from Ossetia earned its own frame on the wall. Someday I'll invite him over for a cocktail, let him thumb through the collection, and then proceed to beat him about the ears with a rolled-up newspaper for dragging the public perception of journalists further down the toilet.

There was a pause on the line as Kailas took a breath, the reporter timidly mumbling something in their defense. It was followed by an explosive continuation of Kailas's tirade. "Deadlines don't mean jack shit to those outside this newsroom, goddamit: not the reader, and not your source. If you sit by and wait for them to call you when they're good and ready for a fucking interview, this is what happens. I don't care how you do it, just fix this. Get another source if you have to, but do it today. Now get out of my office and don't come back until you've got a worthwhile update."

I smiled as Kailas's pitiless tirade came to a conclusion.

"So what are you going to do?" he asked me, his enraged demeanor instantly dropping back to calm and collected.

"Honestly, I don't know. I'm calling from a borrowed sat phone right now—the colonel says they've already shut down access to the Internet and blocked cell signals. I'm going to have to find another way to get you my story."

"You still have any friends in Israel?"

"You mean ones that wouldn't shoot on sight?"

"I'd imagine that would be preferable."

"A few. I'll see if I can get a paper copy out of the country and uploaded to you in a timely fashion."

"That'd be nice."

Growing solemn, I said, "I don't think this is going to be like Korea, Kailas. It's not posturing this time. This is the real deal—there are a whole lot of people pissed off and ready for bloodshed."

"Well, do your best not to get shot. I'm not going to be able to save you from here. We were already warned by the State Department about sending our people over there."

"Understood, but no promises," I said. "Hopefully I'll be in touch."

I ended the call, folded the phone's antenna, and gingerly returned it to the table. Realizing I'd been left completely alone for the first time since my arrival, I peeked around the corner into what must have been the colonel's study. From outside, a soft glow shined through the room's window, passing around tree branches and casting finger-like shadows upon the opposite wall. The room smelled of cigarette smoke covered up by lemon-scented wood polish.

I felt a cold shiver run up my spine as I stepped inside and gently closed the door behind me. I don't get my jollies from rummaging through other people's stuff, but sometimes it's a necessary part of the job.

Journalism is like detective work in that there are long-established moral boundaries and accepted rules to gathering information. But I've found getting to the truth often requires a more forthright approach. A young collegiate journalism student might politely wait by the door and ask the colonel for a formal interview, nod politely at his answers, and stick only to their list of questions. In return, they'd get a prefabricated load of bullshit one hundred percent of the time. Sometimes, it pays to work outside the morally acceptable limitations of investigation, if only for a moment, to get at a truth that would otherwise never be revealed. I look at it like this: If people would simply tell the truth at the onset, I wouldn't need to squeeze the truth out of them by surreptitious means.

Jimmying open Orabi's desk drawers as I tapped his computer awake, I listened over the whir of the hard drive for any approaching movement. Thinking of the handgun on the colonel's hip, it occurred to me that my being here would certainly not set us off on the right foot should he come to investigate.

But no risk, no gain.

The computer's screen refreshed, bringing up a passcode requirement. Flipping the keyboard over, I scanned it for a sticky note or scribbles from a permanent marker revealing the colonel's password. Even in an age when stories of stolen account information and rampant hacking have become commonplace, most people continue to put in minimal effort hiding their security information. The most common password is still 'password', and if that isn't taped to the side of the monitor, keep looking. It's probably within arm's reach.

I set about searching the desk. It was spartan—a single pen, a stapler, one notebook—empty of any notation—three paperclips, and a clear plastic container filled with brass thumbtacks. That was it. Not a single memo, printed email, or report. Not so much as a performance evaluation. Apparently, Orabi preferred to keep his work away from his home—a good policy from a security perspective, but frustrating as hell for my purposes.

I felt his footsteps reverberating along the floorboards before I heard them.

Moving quickly but as quietly as I could muster, I closed the desk drawers, held the computer's power button just long enough to force an abrupt shut down, and searched for a place to hide. The room had no closet or furniture large enough to hide behind, so I dashed toward the window and began fumbling with the latch holding it closed.

The footsteps stopped just outside the door.

Move faster, Grant. Don't look at the door; focus on the window.

I looked back at the room's entrance nervously as I pried at the fastener with my thumb and forefinger, the hallway's light casting shadows of a man's legs through the gap between the door and floor.

I told you not to look at the door.

4

A Meal Fit for a Colonel

My pulse thumping in my ears, I gave a final squeeze. To my relief, with a reluctant squeak, the window frame popped open. Leaping through the narrow aperture between the window's glass and the frame, I took a wide grip on the sill with both hands as my body swung against the building's siding, twenty feet from the ground. I pushed the pane shut just as the room's door slowly opened. A smart man would have stayed perfectly still. Held his breath. Prayed a little. Me? I peeked back up to see who had interrupted my search.

It wasn't the colonel.

Perry scanned the room before setting to work on the desk and starting the computer back up, his feathery blond hair glowing in the monitor's light.

The worthless bastard had unsurprisingly followed my lead. I wasn't mad that he had interrupted my snooping as much as I was that he had copied my style entirely.

No doubt with a devious look on my face, I spread my fingers wide, swung my arm back, and slapped the glass loudly. As though my palm had contacted the side of his face instead of the window, Perry dropped to the floor and skittered into a corner in a wild panic. I let out a low, guttural laugh. Tormenting the poor bastard made setbacks a whole lot easier to take.

Staring at the window aghast, Perry suddenly recognized me and took a deep breath, letting his chin drop to his chest.

"Jesus Christ, Cogar," he mouthed.

Opening the window and staring off into the night sky uncomfortably, he said, "So I guess this is one of those instances where you don't say anything, and neither will I."

"Find anything good in there?" I asked, still smiling at Perry's terrified reaction.

"Someone interrupted me before I got a good look."

"Well, I'll save you some time. There's nothing of any real interest, and the computer's password protected."

"You check under the keyboard?"

I cast him an annoyed look. "First place I looked. I'm not an amateur."

"Just asking. Seems to work most times."

"Did you follow me up here?" I probed, adjusting my grip on the windowsill.

"Why do you always assume I'm following you? I've learned from a few of your techniques over the years, but that doesn't mean I'm just blindly chasing after you. I mean, come on, Cogar; this house is filled with reporters. I'd be surprised if the others aren't sneaking up here as we speak."

No more had he said the last word before someone called down the hallway.

"Mr. Cogar? Mr. Rothko? The colonel would like us in the foyer. Gentlemen?"

More footsteps approached from the hallway.

"Shit, Perry, help me up." I said, my feet scrambling against the building's slick walls.

"There's no time," Perry said over his shoulder as he rushed toward the door. "I'll cover for you until you get back inside." He exited hurriedly and closed the door behind him.

"Perry, you self-serving bastard." I whispered under my breath as I struggled to pull myself back up into the room. Suddenly, my fingers slipped, my chin banged against the window's frame, and I dropped abruptly to the packed earth below. Landing deep in the shrubs as blitzes of sparkling light rushed across my vision, I let out a groan.

One of the guards grunted at the noise, tossed his cigarette into the driveway, and began walking toward me, unfurling his weapon's sling.

The fucker looked mean. Hardened. With an angry stare that said if he caught me sneaking around in the colonel's bushes, he'd more gladly curb stomp me and pretend the fall had killed me than haul me in for questioning.

Slithering flat against the building's foundation under cover of shrubbery, I followed the soldier's boots as they neared my face. I could hear his breathing and smell the fresh cigarette smoke on his clothes. He paused mere feet away. I was as good as caught.

Then, I smelled urine.

Watering the bushes, the guard sighed, relieved. I grimaced and curled my body away from the stream. I resolved to tell the colonel that I'd seen this man dropping trou before one of the lady reporters in attendance as soon as I snuck back into the building. *I don't know what you consider acceptable in your country, Colonel, but from where I come from, that behavior isn't tolerated.*

When the soldier had finished, he shuffled back toward his men, kicking at the dirt as he lit a fresh cigarette. Careful to avoid his puddle, I crawled on hands and knees around the building's corner and, peeking through a window, spotted the other reporters congregating in the room's center. Trying to downplay my shortness of breath, I snuck back to the entryway, keeping a wary eye out for more guards, and strolled back into the foyer just as the colonel began speaking.

"Is everyone here? Excellent. For those interested in a little entertainment before dinner, please come with me."

I followed the crowd, dusting off the dirt from my coat and pants. Leading us down a sweeping marble staircase to a perfectly manicured garden, the colonel snapped his fingers and two men entered carrying a large plastic case on their shoulders. They gently set the package on a nearby bench. Orabi pried open the set of latches, lifted the lid, and removed a suppressed Heckler & Koch MP5 submachine gun.

"Does anyone care to shoot this beauty? How about you, Mr. Rothko? You look like a man with a penchant for shooting."

He handed the weapon to Perry, who clumsily pointing it downrange, obviously unsure how to operate the gun but too proud to admit it in front of his peers.

I speculated why the colonel had brought us out here. Was this meant as subtle intimidation by reminding us of his government's firepower? Or perhaps it was a test to see if one of us might be a little too competent with military-grade weapons to be just a foreign correspondent. Maybe he just had a strange sense of hospitality.

The colonel continued, "It's the same weaponry currently employed by your own military's special operations forces."

"Then why do you have it?" Shouted a short brunette from the front of the crowd. Sally Parker, an infamously obnoxious reporter from the Los Angeles Times, had a voice that could be heard screeching above the din of even the loudest press conference. And, as though she felt a need to prove her competence as a female journalist in a largely male-dominated field, she was often aggressive to the point of malevolence. In the few times we'd met, we didn't get along.

"That's an excellent question, Ms. Parker. Does anyone care to answer her?"

Slipping through the crowd of reporters, I gingerly lifted one of the weapons from the case. "Because, Colonel, the U.S. makes an annual gift of, what, a billion dollars in military aid to Egypt? With that kind of green,

I'm surprised you guys don't hand these out like party favors." Checking the fullness of the magazine before sliding it back into place and racking the submachine gun's forward slide, I turned to Perry and whispered, "Hey, Perry? Safety's on."

He looked down at his weapon confusedly.

Turning my attention to a row of vases the colonel had set before a decorative stone wall for such a purpose, I held the MP5 tight to my hip and squeezed the trigger.

The gun emitted a clattering series of whistles as nine-millimeter slugs collapsed three of the clay vessels in a row. Letting off the trigger, I rolled the selector to SAFE and tossed the weapon into the colonel's open hands as the others clapped hesitantly. They would never have any idea that I was an infamously lousy shot and I was as surprised as they were at my accuracy.

"Very impressive, Mr. Cogar. Clearly, your time on the battlefield has honed your skills."

Perry quietly set his gun on the table.

"Would anyone else care to try? It's really a great deal of fun."

Sally, unwilling to miss an opportunity to voice her opinion, said, "I'll not help reinforce the stereotype that *all*

Americans are trigger-happy lunatics." She said that last bit while staring directly at me.

For a moment, I considered not saying anything. Time has taught me that voicing a contradictory opinion to a belligerent person does little to change their view; it only escalates the situation. But the words slipped out despite my admittedly feeble attempt at restraint.

"No, of course you won't. But you don't seem to have any problem helping them view us as self-righteous and delusional, do you? You must be one of those privileged types who look down on those who, by necessity, use these," I patted the weapon's case, "to earn and protect the same rights you inherited."

"Privileged types?" she said, advancing toward me, her hands balled into fists. "I'll shove my privileged fist up your...."

The colonel stepped between us and smiled. "Perhaps we should move back inside? I believe supper is ready."

She frowned, giving me the dirtiest glare she could muster, turned, and headed for the stairway in a huff.

Perry quickly moved to Sally's side as the crowd moved up the staircase. He wasted no time in whispering how arrogant and wrong I was, and how he admired her courage—and beauty. I just smiled, recalling his terrified reaction when I'd surprised him in Orabi's office.

The colonel stepped up behind me and patted my back; then began rubbing my shoulder, a gesture that gave me an uncomfortable chill. "It seems odd that there would be such contrast in opinions between fellow Americans."

"My country is deeply polarized, sir. You probably know the feeling."

He laughed, but didn't remove his hand from my arm until we reached the top of the stairs. "I most certainly do, Mr. Cogar."

"Colonel, are you married?"

"Why do you ask?"

"Just idle curiosity," I said, rolling my shoulder uncomfortably under his palm.

"I'm married to my work, Mr. Cogar. That's enough for me." Looking over my left hand for a ring, he said, "And that must be the case with you, too."

My face flushed as I stammered, "Not exactly. It's just that none of the women I've been with have found the courage to ask me yet."

Stepping inside, Orabi patted my back a final time before walking to the front of the crowd, guiding us to a sweeping table beneath a large crystal chandelier in the mansion's dining room. A tuxedoed man seated before a gloss-black Steinway piano touched his forefinger to his tongue and began sweeping through a well-worn booklet full of musical notation. Watching the other reporters take their seats, I motioned to a server nearby.

"Excuse me, you wouldn't happen to have hot sauce or some kind of spicy pepper you could add to my meal, would you? I lost my taste buds in the war." The woman nodded and smiled politely as she turned toward the kitchen. "I mean *really* hot. Okay?" I called after her.

Grabbing a seat directly across from Perry, I nodded at him and smiled. He returned the gesture, but his eyes reflected his bewilderment. He just couldn't seem to figure me out. Most times, I made it abundantly clear I couldn't stand to be near him. Then, as if I'd suffered a sudden schizophrenic episode, I became his closest friend. Of course, those episodes always preceded some practical joke or other unfortunate accident befalling Mr. Rothko. He just hadn't put two and two together yet.

Within minutes, steaming plates of lamb and lentils were set before us, utensils of pure silver lining either side. The pungent steam rising from my dish burned my nose and made my eyes water. My rival unfolded his napkin, laying it across his lap, before selecting a fork from his left.

"Perry, have you ever seen a tapestry like that one?" I said kindly, motioning to embroidery behind him. As he craned his neck to see what I was talking about, I dexterously substituted his meal with my own.

"I guess not," he said, turning back toward me. "Why?"

"I haven't either. I just found it interesting. I've been all over the world, but I've never seen one quite like that one."

"Yeah, I suppose."

The room grew quiet, the pianist folding his hands in his lap as the colonel took his seat at the head of the table. Holding his hands out before him with palms cupped toward the ceiling, Orabi prayed, "*Bismillahi wa 'ala baraka-tillah.*" Raising his balding head, he looked at me and grinned. "Would you care to say a prayer honoring your god, Mr. Cogar?"

I glanced around the table at the expectant faces of my fellow reporters before slipping my fork under a pile of lentils. "I think you about covered it." I didn't appreciate being singled out, particularly when it came to prayer. My god and I have an understanding—we don't talk outside active warzones.

Orabi laughed loudly in reply—far more forceful than was appropriate given the circumstances. The laugh quickly turned to a chuckle, the chuckle to a kind of throaty cough. "Well, I'm sure at this point you're all decidedly curious about the reason I've invited you here this evening. Undoubtedly you've come to Egypt with certain preconceptions about the government and the insurrections that have been taking place. I wanted to ensure you receive a balanced perspective."

"That's very thoughtful, Colonel," Sally said politely.

Oh come on. He's not doing it as a kindness; this is damage control you vacuous bitch.

Perry eyed her hungrily as he carved away a piece of lamb, poked it with his fork, and moved it toward his lips.

"I'll be the first to concede that our country has deep-seated issues," the colonel continued. "Though we've done our best to mitigate the levels of poverty, over-population, and lack of education here, those issues are still a concern. But, though there are many citizens who feel that their voice has not been heard or that their government is too free in exercising authority, they only have the luxury of such criticism because we provide those same citizens with a safe environment in which they can thrive."

Blatant lie of the evening numero uno.

Though I'll openly admit that I'm not an expert on current events in every corner of the world, I'm not some Hawaiian-shirt wearing retiree on my first senior cruise, either. I'd done my fair share of research prior to my arrival in Cairo, sent a few inquisitive emails to old contacts in the region, and I've spent more than a small portion of my life in the Middle East. I wasn't completely clueless about what was going on, even if the colonel thought otherwise. His approach to 'explaining' the situation here felt cheap, rehearsed, and a teeny bit condescending.

"So this will probably be quick to pass?" Perry asked, his cheeks growing red as he reached for his glass.

That's the most probing question you've got, you sycophantic maggot?

"The protests? Oh yes. They are little more than juvenile cries for attention. And like a child, if given the time needed to cry and kick their feet, they'll exhaust themselves and be happier for it. My job is simply to keep them from hurting themselves in the process."

Lie number two. Let it go, Cogar; you've got nothing to prove here. This is neither the time nor the place to start calling people out on bullshit. I just needed to get through the evening without making any new enemies or becoming labeled as a threat to the state. Slipping the pad of my thumb over my pointer finger's middle knuckle, I pushed down until it cracked; then began moving down the line to my other fingers. It wasn't like my contradicting the colonel was going to change anything, anyway. In quintessential military fashion, Orabi viewed the protests only as an act of insubordination that could be strong-armed back into compliance. Once squelched, the city would return to normal, if only with minor modifications to keep the population in check in the future. But there was a problem with his plan: The people were aggressively pursuing a democracy for the first time in the nation's history, and even if they didn't succeed this time, they would continue trying until they got it. And when they did get it, he would find that easily the most dangerous transition a country familiar with a long-standing dictatorship can face is an abrupt one to democracy. It has a splintering effect where religious, military, and business entities that used to play by the same rules—the rules of the dictator—get shattered into smaller special-interest groups that believe only in doing things their way. And because they are used to laws enforced by guns, they set forth to make their own in similar fashion. Criminals and terrorists thrive. Something ugly resembling full-blown anarchy typically follows. There are exceptions to this rule, obviously, but this seems to be the typical outcome.

"Well that's comforting to know it'll be over soon," said the heavyset Filipino reporter from the *Orlando Sentinel* as he ripped a fist-sized piece of bread from a loaf and stuffed it into his cheek.

Perry coughed as he bumped his chest with a closed fist. Though he was suffering, and clearly confused why he was the only one who was, my rival was trying his damnedest to keep a straight face—nodding and smiling as the other reporter continued, crumbled bits of bread dribbling from his open mouth. "I know I speak for everyone when I say it's deeply troubling to think fellow countrymen would be forced to fight each other."

"Over and done with within the week, I can assure you, ladies and gentlemen," Orabi replied as he carefully carved away a thin slice of lamb. *Lie three. That tears it.*

I waited a moment for someone to protest the colonel's obvious bias and dismissal of the violence at hand. No one said a word—either through apathy, prudence, or agreement. I shook my head and spoke up, quietly at first.

"Colonel, I can't shake the feeling that you're not giving a fair assessment of the severity of this rebellion or those social issues you mentioned earlier."

"Really? And why's that?" the colonel said, feigning interest as he tipped forward a porcelain gravy boat filled with tahini sauce, smothering everything on his plate.

"Well, first, you make it sound as though these people have no reason to protest. I haven't been in the country long, but it doesn't take a terribly observant person to notice how many people here are living in squalor," I said, tapping my pointer finger on the rim of my crystal glass. "And, not to make this too personal, but you have a lovely home here, and it's pretty hard to miss that squad of soldiers you have pulling private security out front to protect it. The distance between you, a government official, and the average citizen is pretty noticeable."

"Had they maintained an exemplary military record for twenty years and shed blood for their country, they too would have these luxuries."

"I find that unlikely, but okay. Assuming that were the case, there are still an overwhelming majority of Egyptians who are barely scratching out a living here. If they aren't allowed to complain about their situation without getting hauled off to prison, and can't cast a meaningful vote against the current regime in your 'elections,' you have to acknowledge the fact that their frustration is going to turn violent."

My voice reflected my irritability. I hadn't had a drink since getting off the plane several hours prior, and I never got the cup of coffee I was holding out for. It was beginning to show. Though I'm convinced I don't have an addictive personality, my body doesn't seem to recognize that.

The colonel cleared his throat uncomfortably. "This is why I wanted to speak with you before you write your respective articles. Mr. Cogar has illustrated a typical foreigner's perspective of the state of affairs here—one that couldn't be farther from the truth. Like a disease that spreads, the rebellions we've faced are fueled by lies uttered by President Mubarak's political opposition.

Extremist religious groups such as the Muslim Brotherhood incite riots to destabilize our country in efforts to make it a terrorist breeding ground—much like Afghanistan has become. You've spent some time in Afghanistan, haven't you, Mr. Cogar?"

Perry drained his glass and was now motioning to the server for more water.

"Yes, I have," I sighed, biting my lip as I scanned through memories of the snow-capped mountains, the violent dust storms, and the soldiers I'd interviewed that had come back missing limbs or hadn't come back at all. I was suddenly angry that Orabi had brought it up. "And like the U.S. did with the Mujahideen during their fight against the Russians in the '80s, they've strategically backed the Egyptian government instead of those pesky fundamentalist Muslim groups—the enemy of my enemy and all that," I replied. "But that still doesn't explain why those groups can show up and turn your entire country on end. Extremism only thrives in places where the average citizen has become so dissatisfied, they'd do anything to change the status quo."

The colonel leaned in, sliding aside his plate, and propped his elbows on the table. "Again, Mr. Cogar, I'm not dismissing the fact that we have a few social issues to confront, but which country doesn't? Surely, even the United States has its fair share of poverty-stricken and disenfranchised parties."

"The difference is, Colonel, we don't make a habit of beating our poor to death in the streets for protesting peacefully," I said deliberately.

I regretted that last part before it even left my mouth.

The pianist stopped mid-measure.

Sitting up straight in his chair as though I'd just kicked him in the shin, the colonel stayed quiet for a moment, looking both irritated and confused. Perry stared at me, wide-eyed. He looked comical—his eyes bloodshot, his nose running, and his face the color of a ripe tomato.

"That's hardly any way to treat your host," the reporter from the Daily News said stuffily. *Well it certainly can't compare with the treatment your wife would be giving him under the table if she were here, if that's what you meant.*

"Typical. Such an asshole." Sally added.

"No harm meant by it," I said cheerfully, folding the cloth napkin in my lap and placing it over my half-eaten meal. I'd lost my appetite. "I thought we were having a friendly conversation. After all," I said, sliding my glass of water toward Perry, who accepted it gratefully, "what fun would it be if we agreed on everything?"

"Quite so, Mr. Cogar. Tonight has been nothing if not stimulating." Dabbing the corners of his mouth with his napkin, Orabi pushed his seat back and stood, gesturing for the pianist to continue. "Ladies and gentlemen, though I understand you may have existing plans for sleeping arrangements during your time in Cairo, I'd like to personally pay for your stay at the Conrad Cairo. I think it would be easier to ensure your collective safety if you were all in the same hotel. I'll have guards posted to ensure you'll have a secure place to stay in case things get out of hand." While the other reporters stupidly expressed their gratitude for the colonel's ostensible concern for their health, I knew it was a thinly veiled attempt to keep us herded together and under watch. He was clearly determined to keep every foreign journalist he could firmly under his thumb.

"Please, everyone, enjoy some dessert and feel free to make my home your own." Turning to me, he said, "Mr. Cogar, would you mind joining me in my study, please?"

I nearly jumped. There are days where I lose control over which thoughts are kept in my mind and which ones slip out of my mouth. Had I just voiced my doubts about the colonel's intentions aloud? Reluctantly following the officer down the familiar hallway leading to his study, I began to grow anxious—why did he only invite me? Did he know I'd been rummaging through his office? I envisioned him motioning me into the room with a smile, withdrawing his sidearm, and assassinating me on the spot. Suddenly remembering Orabi's conduct in the garden, I began wondering if perhaps his intentions were decidedly more...sexual in nature. Considering that, I quickly resolved that I'd prefer the assassination.

"Please, have a seat," he said as he tugged the pull cord on a stained-glass floor lamp and motioned to a set of wingback chairs. Between them sat an ivory chess set I hadn't noticed before. "Can I serve you a drink?"

I raised an eyebrow. Drinking in Egypt was largely a tourist activity; the country is overwhelmingly comprised of Sunni Muslims who don't consume alcohol.

"That's not very Muslim of you."

"I'm not very Muslim, Mr. Cogar."

"But your prayer at dinner..."

"Smoke and mirrors, my friend. In my line of work, it's wise not to attract attention to your personal life or its eccentricities—in this case, my absence of religious affiliation. Bourbon?"

"Absolutely."

I began to relax. If he was going to kill me, at least he had the grace to give me a drink, first. I watched as he carefully poured a small amount into two crystal snifters.

"I suppose you're wondering why I asked you to join me here."

"Particularly after our talk over dinner. I would have thought you'd prefer to have me shot than have a drink with me."

He laughed quietly. "I'm not so easy to offend, Mr. Cogar. But it's interesting that you mention our little discussion—that is, to some extent, why you're here. As I'm sure you know, journalists are unique creatures," he said, offering me my drink.

"I'm flattered."

He continued without looking at me, "Reporters, as I view them, are little more than a town gossip with a salary. Most, like a pig after a truffle, root about, shoving their noses in the dirt in search of a story to send back to the uneducated-but-passionate masses."

I didn't like where he was going with this.

"They have no interest in a story aside from how it will be received by their countrymen. If they could help crucify Jesus Christ himself in exchange for being the first to publish a story on it, they'd do so without remorse."

"Harsh."

"But true. Those men and women out there," he motioned toward the dining room, "are piranhas, Mr. Cogar. They would sooner see my country burn for the sake of a story than have our culture, our way of life, preserved." He took a hurried sip from his glass.

I can see why you'd want to preserve your way of life, you wealthy bastard. I had no illusions about how a military officer like Orabi had come into such affluence; it wasn't by being frugal, that's for damn sure. More likely, he was a member of Mubarak's intimate coterie, one of the privileged good old boys at the top enjoying the fruit of the nation's labor and working only to exterminate those who might jeopardize the sweet gig he had going.

"They go out of their way to exacerbate existing problems," Orabi continued as he chewed off a hangnail. "But you, Mr. Cogar—despite your probing questions at dinner, your entire persona tells me you aren't interested in scandal or simply regurgitating a tale of rebels and their fight against an 'evil' empire. You sincerely care about getting the facts, and you desire to give a balanced perspective. I respect that a great deal."

I set my glass down and pushed a pawn forward on the chessboard. I have a peculiar way of playing the game: A former diplomat friend of mine once showed me a series of moves known as the 'Scholar's Checkmate' where a player could win in just four moves. Some careless opponents fall for it, most don't. If I can't win in those first moves, my strategy devolves into a clumsy slugfest I usually lose. This is probably telling of my character. But it's also revealing of my opponent's character. "I'll be the first to say that I'm no moralist, Colonel. But if there's one thing I've always considered sacred, it's my reporting: Accuracy and fairness take precedence."

The colonel pushed a pawn to confront mine. "That's very honorable, and very rare." Sliding his foot towards mine slyly, the officer stared hard at the chess pieces as though such an advance was a merely subconscious effort.

"I'd like to think it's not so rare," I replied, moving my feet a similar distance away from Orabi. "Maybe the work of a few bad reporters has tarnished the reputation of the rest."

I scooted my bishop halfway across the board.

"Optimistic, I'm afraid. And I would ordinarily say that optimism is dangerous for a man in your line of work, but then I've seen the way you handle a gun. Instead, maybe you are one of those rare idealists who have somehow avoided becoming jaded despite years of experience." He moved a knight from behind his line of pawns.

"You clearly don't know me very well, Colonel," I said, thumbing my queen across the board. The officer pushed another knight forward cautiously in response. "I've seen enough of the world to know it's a ruthless, wicked place. Even though my writing won't change mankind's capacity for evil, I still hope it gives a voice to those who deserve it."

Orabi watched me as I finished my glass of whiskey—the amber spirits forging a simmering trail down my throat—set it down, and smacked my lips. Waiting a few seconds for him to see that my next move would end the game in a checkmate, I said, "Are you sure you wanted to make that last move?"

5

One Hell of a Strange Day

An hour later, after I'd reclaimed my bag from the phone stand and rejoined the other reporters, Orabi escorted us outside to a row of waiting taxis. I shuffled my jacket over my shoulders, thankful to be leaving. After my outburst at dinner, my peers had begun avoiding me as though I were the only passenger on a packed metro with a bad case of whooping cough.

"I hope you've all enjoyed dinner, and I wish you a pleasant night. Should you have any questions or find yourselves in need of an armed escort at any point during your stay here in Egypt," Orabi gestured over his shoulder at the guards, each man eyeing us with a look of contempt, "please don't hesitate to contact me immediately." He turned to me as the crowd of reporters dispersed and offered his hand. "Mr. Cogar, it's been a rare pleasure." In his palm perched a business card. He slipped it into mine as he shook my hand.

"Should you wish to meet at some point in a more private capacity," he said, "that's my personal line."

"I appreciate the gesture, Colonel. But I've no doubt we'll be seeing more of each other in the next few days, whether we intend to or not."

"Intriguing."

It wasn't meant to be.

"Have a good evening, sir. And thanks for dinner and the entertainment. Practice up on that chessboard for next time." Even though Orabi's and my perspectives on most everything seemed to clash, I always make a point to leave on a good note, even with those I perceive to be antagonistic to my work. As a rule, I try to reserve judgment until I get back home and the article's been published. In my line of work, it's not uncommon for the bad guys at breakfast to become the good guys by dinner.

I eagerly climbed into the last open taxi, ready to go back to my hotel room, take a long shower, and fall asleep cradling a bottle of whatever regional alcoholic beverage I could scrounge, only to find myself seated beside Sally and Perry.

Apparently the other reporters thought it best to leave Satan and Hitler their own car.

For half an hour, I could feel Sally's glare on my skin as I rested my head against the window and admired Cairo's brightly lit skyline. Casting an occasional glance at her to make sure I wasn't being paranoid, I found that she wouldn't avert her stare—her eyes locked furiously to mine until I looked away.

You'd think I kicked her dog.

I didn't like making enemies, particularly among people I might someday end up sharing a bunker with or needing a favor from. But it seemed to me that her reaction, considering what little I'd actually said, was completely overblown; had she listened to even one casual conversation between Kailas and myself, she would gain a profound appreciation for how offensive I can really be.

When the taxi finally rolled up to the Conrad Cairo, I opened the door before the vehicle had fully stopped—the smell of exhaust and gasoline hanging on the night air—and made a beeline for the lobby. An elderly gentleman, wearing a hotel staffer's uniform and an expression so stoic he could have passed for part of the décor, waited with a dozen small envelopes, containing what I hoped were our room keys, in his outstretched, gloved palm. He handed me one and nodded his head knowingly. No doubt he, too, shared my disdain for the crowd of reporters beginning to mill about the building's entrance.

Jogging past the elevators, I swung open the door to the stairwell and headed for the fourth floor. Matching the room number on the door to the one hastily scratched on the envelope in my hand, I slipped inside, closed the door, and sat down on the edge of the bed. It wasn't the kind of room I would have asked for normally—I typically prefer an inside room on the second or third floor if one's available. Such a location gives you a buffer from the outside, reducing your chances of catching a stray bullet or shrapnel while you sleep. It's high enough to avoid thrown objects from ground level, but low enough to make it to an exit before the building collapses. The room I was in gave a great view, but offered none of the protection. Like so many other times in my life, I would just hope for the best and try to enjoy the ride.

Thump, thump, thump.

"For fuck's sake," I said under my breath as I pushed myself to my feet and grudgingly moved back toward the door. It was probably the hotel staff coming to tell me I had rushed past the sign-in process and needed to return to the lobby. Opening the door a crack, I found myself eye-to-eye with Sally as she pushed her way inside.

"I've got something I need to say to you, Cogar. Right now."

Undoubtedly still hot under the collar about my statements over dinner, Sally had, rather than continue on blissfully hating me in private, decided I needed to be confronted.

"Look, I'm really not in the mood to argue right now. Can it wait until tomorrow, or maybe the end of time? I know, why don't you write your thoughts down and slide the note under the door when you're done? That way we both get what we want."

Grabbing my collar with both hands, the short brunette pulled me against her lips; then jumped from the floor and wrapped her legs around my waist.

"What are you doing?" I managed to say out of the corner of my mouth as her tongue played across my teeth. Falling backwards and slamming against the bathroom door, I struggled to extricate her body from mine.

Finally coming up for air, she said, "Take me."

"What? Why would I do that?"

Dropping her legs to the floor and pushing me into the bed, she tore her shirt open, the buttons breaking free and bouncing on the carpet, and leapt atop me. Grabbing my wrists, she shoved my hands against her breasts and began gyrating her hips violently against mine.

"I said take me."

Though not altogether unattractive, her demeanor and our history as antagonists left me decidedly un-roused. And though I had enjoyed enough angry lovemaking sessions in my life to know that sexual encounters with a frustrated woman could be a wild, heart-stopping experience, I couldn't bring myself to feel anything but confusion at the current situation.

A knock at the door pulled her attention away from biting my neck and tugging my pants down my thighs. Looking down at me with a raised eyebrow, she slapped my face sharply and muttered, "you disgust me," before crossing her arms and walking out. Perry, standing on the other side of the doorway, took on a confused look that mirrored my own upon seeing the scantily clad reporter exit my room.

"I came by to talk to you about dinner," he said distractedly, his eyes following her down the hall. "But I think it can wait for another time."

"I'd appreciate that. It's been one hell of a strange day," I said, motioning to Perry to close the door. He stopped midway out and stepped back inside.

"I'm sorry, but Cogar, I got the impression when we were back in Shanghai that you're pissed at me about something. I know we've had our differences over the years, but I'd like to put all those to rest sometime," he said, staring at the floor and tapping his finger against his leg, his hands in his pockets.

I was utterly taken aback. Horrified even. My rival, the man whose face I had superimposed on my dartboard at home, was offering me an olive branch. I wasn't prepared for that.

"You and I really aren't so different, you know? I mean, meeting in the colonel's study like that…" he chuckled. "Great minds think alike, right? We both love reporting, and we've been in the game for a long time. It's just…it would be nice to have an ally out there. You know, someone to watch my back."

His appeal for friendship actually drove me to anger. Just because he had inexplicably sprouted the slightest inkling of human decency didn't mean I was going to suddenly disregard the last decade of ill feelings I'd harbored toward the bastard and become buddies. That's not something that goes away overnight.

"I don't know what you're talking about Perry. Things are exactly the way they've always been."

"I know, and I'd like to change that. I'm offering you my apologies for the way I've behaved around you, and I was hoping you'd be a big enough man to accept them and maybe acknowledge that you've been less than kind to me, too."

"Perry, I don't know if you're looking for some kind of Kumbaya session here or what, but I can tell you this much: You're barking up the wrong tree. First, yes I am still pissed about Darfur and still pissed about Shanghai and still pissed about every other stop along the way where you've managed to interfere with my work, make me look bad, or get me into more trouble than I could have possibly asked for. Second: We are *very* different. Very. Different. The indisputable fact of the matter is, when it comes to writing and reporting, you're a two-bit hack—a panderer to the masses. Your target demographic is comprised of people incapable of wiping their own asses and would have succumbed to natural selection if it weren't for the advent of modern medicine and lower public-school standards. It confounds me not only that you work for such a prestigious publication, but that they haven't caught on to your inordinate lack of skill and booted your ass out the door yet."

I felt a pinch of guilt as I berated him, but pushed it away and let the anger roll through me. I finally had a good opportunity to take him to task for the years of trouble he'd given me. "I don't know what angle you're playing by coming here and apologizing. Frankly, I don't care. You've fooled me once by playing nice, and I'll be damned if you catch me with my pants down again."

We both looked down at my unbelted pants.

"Figuratively."

Perry, face red and eyes downcast, clenched his jaw and mumbled, "Have a good night, Cogar."

As the door closed behind him, I tugged my pants back up angrily. I felt like a real jackass for being so hostile to Perry, but given our history together, I just knew he had to be up to something.

Turning to look out my room's window, I took in a sweeping panorama of the almost disappointingly metropolitan city—brightly lit freeways weaving around enormous but unimaginatively rectangular skyscrapers crowned by broad neon signs and digital screens flashing advertisements. It seemed as though the more I saw of the world, the more difficult it became to ignore the similarities rendering it all just one homogenous blur. This was my first time in Egypt, and so far, it had proved to be nothing memorable.

This struck me as especially disappointing.

COGAR'S REVOLT

Egypt had been the source of so many of my boyhood fantasies, and the thought of exploring tombs, discovering lost treasure, and fighting off my competition with a bullwhip while wearing a fedora and driving a stolen Nazi Kübelwagen was just as appealing now as it had ever been. But looking through the glass at the staggered building tops and listening to the muted honks of car horns as they rose from the streets, I resigned myself to accept that this was bound to be just another assignment like all the rest.

6

A Roll of the Dice

The next morning, I rolled out of bed early. *Really* early. The warm, golden rays of the Egyptian sun hadn't even risen to the tops of the city's lowest buildings yet. Another side effect of perpetual travel—one's body constantly fights to adjust to new time zones. That, combined with the din and light from the protests in Tahrir Square a few miles away and my equally riotous bowel movements—resulting from what I could only attribute to the meal I'd consumed the previous evening, the one intended for Perry—had managed to keep me awake for most of the night. Though I was feeling a little better after a long shower, I quietly prayed to whichever gods watch over unlucky travelers that it was just food poisoning and not a parasite or cholera. Been there, and let me tell you, death is preferable. Unfortunately, even making a habit of drinking only bottled water in countries without a potable water supply doesn't promise you'll stay healthy—restaurants, hotels, and local vendors still cook and make their coffee using water from the tap. Usually, you just say a little prayer, toss back another dose of antibiotics and a shot of strong liquor, and hope for the best.

Stuffing my toothbrush in my cheek, I checked my phone, slapped my ruggedized laptop awake, and began pulling my pants on. The colonel hadn't been kidding about the interference: no phone service, no Internet. I found that oddly discomforting, which was a sign that I'd grown too reliant upon technology over the years. It's an easy trap to fall into—the immediacy and almost limitless connectivity electronic devices offer make giving and receiving information from anywhere in the world effortless—even from the bottom of an artillery shell crater. But those devices, no matter their quality, are prone to malfunction, hindered by battery life, and given to complete system failure when struck with bullets and shell fragments. As a young, poor reporter fresh out of Chicago, I used little more than a clunky, bulletproof voice recorder powered by half a dozen AA batteries and a pad of paper on my first battlefield assignments. I'd laughed at other reporters rendered helpless and distraught by a non-functioning computer or phone. Now here I was.

I tucked a small notebook and a pen bearing the hotel's name into my chest pocket. *Guess we're going old school today.*

Stretching my back as I moved before a window overlooking the gently flowing Nile, I resolved to get out of the hotel and explore the city. If I played my cards right, I'd be able to find some disorderly action before it got completely out of hand—with time enough to get quotations from a few of the participants.

Sliding open the zipper on my bag, I stuffed my laptop between the layers of clothes. Even though I intended to take full advantage of the colonel's offer of the free hotel stay for at least a few days more, as a personal rule, I always keep my things packed and ready to grab and go in a hurry. Experience has taught me that the few minutes it takes to collect one's shit and get the hell out of Dodge can make the difference between making it to the embassy safely and getting crushed beneath the crumbling foundation of a hotel hammered by mortar fire. Reporters I've traveled with and the women who have shared my bed tend to view this anticipatory packing as an oddity bordering on paranoia. But most of them don't have firsthand experience in digging themselves out from under a collapsed building, either.

I set my bag inside the bathroom vanity. When visiting an autocratic country where the certainty of being watched or tailed is high—and I knew that Colonel Orabi fit the profile of one who would give such an order to great detail—you can pretty much plan on having your bag searched at some point during your stay. When you get back to your hotel room and find your underwear stuffed in the wrong pocket, it probably wasn't the maid looking for your wallet. Hiding my bag didn't promise to keep that from happening, I just didn't want to make it easy for whoever came looking.

Leaving the TV on to give the illusion that I'd be sticking around and slipping the 'Do not disturb' placard over the door handle, I peeked my head into the hallway, looking for the guards the colonel had tasked with babysitting us. I knew there were two of them at either entrance—I'd checked before I'd gone to sleep the night before—but the hallway appeared clear, and I stepped out.

"Where are you off to so early?"

I froze mid step. Looking to my left, I spotted the reporter from the BBC as he stepped from his room and into the hallway with only his bathrobe on and a toothbrush gripped in his right hand. His narrow features, dotted with freckles, reflected his suspicion as he eyed me. The sharp downward curve of his eyes toward his temples and his receding hairline made his broad forehead seem even larger; his thin, small mouth stayed firmly closed as he awaited my response.

I had only an instant to either lie to the man or trust that he was as suspicious of Colonel Orabi's generosity as I was, and boldly tell him I was leaving. I opted for the latter.

"I'm getting the fuck outta here. What do you have planned for today? Room service and a movie?" I could smell the cheap hotel shampoo emanating from his hair, and I briefly wondered if years of bargain shopping for hair products had been partly responsible for his exposed scalp.

"I plan to wait a bit before attempting to venture out," the reporter said cautiously. "Seems to me that the colonel is unusually concerned with keeping us safe—so much so that he won't let us leave the building at all. Naturally, I can't abide by that; I've got work to do."

I smiled, relieved. "Good to hear that coming from another journo's lips. I was beginning to think I was the only one of us who saw the colonel's benevolence for what it really was."

"I think most of the others know, too. Some are just afraid to end up on Orabi's angry side, and in the case of the new reporters, afraid to get caught up in the violence. But unless the colonel is prepared to physically enforce our staying, he'll have a tough time preventing the rest of us from leaving."

As I stood there nodding in agreement, it suddenly occurred to me that I didn't remember the man's name. Oddly enough, it was his son's name that came to mind immediately. Apparently my brain is better geared to remembering drug dealers than it is respected members of the journalistic community. That should probably concern me.

"How's your son Morgan doing? Out of rehab yet?"

The man's shoulders slumped visibly as he rubbed his eyebrows with his thumb and index finger.

"He was. The police just caught the little blighter again a week ago. Back to prison again. I'm beginning to think he's most comfortable when he's behind bars."

"Damn shame."

"It really is. So much potential wasted." Sighing, the Brit turned and headed back toward his room. "Best of luck in your pursuits, Mr. Cogar. Maybe I'll meet you out there."

Waiting until he'd closed his door, I pried off my shoe, reached beneath the insole, and withdrew a few folded notes I'd withdrawn from an ATM the night before. It's an old trick I picked up when I'd fallen asleep on a train after spending two sleepless days on the bullet-riddled streets of Monrovia during the Second Liberian Civil War. I awoke to find that some unscrupulous passenger had, rather than risk waking me by reaching into my pockets, simply cut them open with a razor blade. They'd taken every last cent I had on my person. It wasn't very much, but it was all I had. That was a hard lesson.

Thumbing through the cash as I jogged down the stairs, I contemplated how effective an attempt at bribing the guards outside would be. Money, as I understood it, went a long way toward getting just about anything you wanted here—so long as the person you're attempting to bribe is one of the unscrupulous kind. Of course, if you happen to guess wrong and make such an offer to a forthright soldier or policeman, the consequence of your unaccepted bribe could mean weeks or months in an Egyptian prison, beatings and torture gratis.

But my options were limited at this point, and I needed to escape the hotel if I was to get anything done during my stay here. I could only hope that the guards were both unprincipled and cheap. I resolved to offer the sentries the little money I had—as gifts to their families and for their hard work keeping us safe, of course—and, if it became necessary, do like Bob Hope and Bing Crosby and give them the paddy-cake routine: distract them with my boyish charm, wallop 'em in the face, and make a run for it. I took a few shallow, excited breaths, then made for the door. Stepping into the outside air fully prepared to recite the very diplomatic conversation starters I'd dreamt up, I spotted the two guards ten feet away—backs turned to me as they lit their cigarettes and stared inattentively at the passing traffic.

Gently shutting the door behind me, I began casually, but urgently, walking away.

Who needs skill when you've got luck like mine?

When I'd made it a few blocks away, I looked over my shoulder to ensure I wasn't being followed before taking in my surroundings. Mature palm trees lining the street swayed gently as a cool breeze rustled my hair. Because it was early in the day and early in the year, the characteristically oppressive Egyptian heat was absent, and it was, in fact, a little chilly for my liking. Partially hidden by the haze of the morning mist, sand-colored buildings—some of modern construction and others relics of centuries past—stood against the horizon. The *Muezzins'* pre-dawn call to prayer boomed from loudspeakers dangling from the underside of minarets— spiraled growths protruding from the rooftops of mosques scattered about the city.

Carefully navigating the already-chaotic, traffic-filled streets, I caught the scent of fresh bread amidst a bouquet of car exhaust and sewage. My stomach grumbled as I followed the smell. Turning down an alleyway between two apartment complexes, suddenly I was in a thriving marketplace. Looking at the smiling faces of the shop owners and the customers beginning their day, I found it hard to believe that the country was really in the midst of the violent, uproarious rioting that had kept me awake the night before.

"You look lost." A woman's voice called out over the din.

Scanning the crowd, my eyes met hers as she stood behind the counter of a market stall. Her face, though partially covered with an olive drab *hijab*, was that of a young woman, not a day over twenty, and cute. She had beautiful green eyes that immediately caught my attention and held it like steel hooks plunged beneath my skin.

"You're probably right; that's how I spend most of my time. What gave me away?"

"Your wandering pace and your very nice suit. Tourist?" she asked, leaning over her booth. Behind her, brightly painted bowls and plates lined the wall and sat in tall stacks near her feet. Apple-scented tobacco smoke drifted on the air, migrating from the mouths of bearded men seated in a circle and smoking a *hookah* nearby.

"In a manner of speaking."

"Journalist, then."

"You caught me," I said, extending my hand over the counter. "My name's Grant. You speak English beautifully."

She looked at my hand curiously.

"Right, sorry. Pleasure to meet you, nonetheless." I'd momentarily forgotten that shaking a woman's hand was a verboten practice in Islam.

"Aqiylah Ibrahim. My father taught me—he spent most of his career in the United States. Where are you from?"

"Chicag…"

Before I could reply, half a dozen children, ranging in age from their early teens to barely old enough to speak, surrounded me, hands held out as they tugged on my pant leg and chattered in Arabic.

"Look guys, I don't have anything you want. Really."

Shouting from her place behind the booth, Aqiylah held out a hand and rolled her pointer finger in a 'come-closer' fashion to the ragtag gang. One of the youngest stared up at me, still tugging on my jacket as her companions moved toward the market stall.

"You heard her," I coaxed.

With lightning speed, the little shit swung an open hand into my groin—a sudden surprising wave of pain scarpering along my pelvis and anchoring in the base of my gut—before dashing away and disappearing among the children crowded tight around the booth.

Aqiylah tried to hide a laugh behind her hand as she asked, "Grant, are you okay?"

Fighting my way back to standing and breathing deeply as the sharp pain slowly ebbed from my right gonad, I mustered a stiff smile and groaned, "Welcome to Egypt, right?"

She looked at me apologetically before turning back to the children. "That wasn't a very nice thing to do. What do you all say to Grant?"

"Sorry!" they all shouted in unison.

"Good," she said. "Now what do you say to me?" she asked, reaching beneath the counter and withdrawing a handful of chocolate candies. Their eyes lit up.

"Please!"

"Good."

As she handed them over, the children squealed with delight and turned to leave. The eldest boy leaned over the stall and whispered in Aqiylah's ear before turning to join the rest of the group. She grabbed him by his shirt collar.

"Mohammed, go buy bread and vegetables," Aqiylah said, stuffing a wad of Egyptian pound notes into his hand. "Everyone gets some."

He began thanking her in Arabic, but she held up a hand, "English."

The boy worked through the words, "Sank you, Aqiylah," before running off to join the others.

I felt a strange, dusty emotion stir inside me— nothing to do with my injured testicle. Images I'd long sequestered of cold, lonely nights on the streets of Chicago played through my head as clearly as if I'd only just experienced them. I often told myself that my life growing up in orphanages and later, sleeping in public library bathrooms, had shaped me to be the man I was today; it had left me with a unique resilience to life's trials and rendered me impervious to the migratory lifestyle of an international news journalist. But it wasn't a childhood I would have wished on anyone.

I'd been lucky—Kailas took me under his wing as a teenager and gave me a sense of purpose and optimism, honing my writing and investigative skills and tempering my attitude. Seeing these kids, damned to a life of bare survival or worse, burned deeply in a part of me I strived to keep hidden from the world—even if one of them had tried to neuter me via blunt force trauma.

Stepping closer to the booth, I said quietly, "If everyone in the world were a little more like you, I think I'd be out of a job."

Aqiylah shook her head. "I don't understand."

"Well, let's just say I don't get sent to cover good news very often. It's refreshing to see someone doing good things—gives me a little hope for the human race."

She shrugged and smiled. "These kids just need a chance. I wish I could give them more. Outside of slipping them a little money for food and teaching them to speak English, I really can't do much for them."

"I take it the language part comes in handy for catering to tourists and the like?"

She grinned. "And the like."

"How about translating?"

"Certainly helpful for translating."

"Have you ever considering working as a translator?"

"Haven't given it a lot of thought," she said. "The opportunity hasn't presented itself yet."

"Well consider it presented. I could use your help: I need someone who speaks the language and knows the locale."

"How much are you paying?" Aqiylah asked abruptly as she swept away a layer of dirt from the countertop with the back of her hand.

I smiled and fingered the rim of a ceramic bowl filled with dried dates.

"Why don't we discuss rates over a cup of coffee?"

When it comes to finding reliable, credible sources in a foreign country, having a talented, honest translator and guide on your side is a godsend. They know their environment and the people who inhabit it better than a foreigner ever could, and they can sense when things are going awry and can communicate exactly when it's time to beat a hasty retreat. While much of my competition would, by necessity, stick to interviewing government officials and accessible English-speaking hotel workers, I'd be plunging into the depths of the authentic Egypt.

It didn't hurt that she was a good-looking woman, either.

She paused, folding her hands as she looked at me with a gaze tinged with uncertainty. After a moment, she said, "I only drink tea. But there's an *ahwa* up the street; I'll take you."

Casually shouting at the man in the next stall that she was leaving, Aqiylah tossed her legs over the front of the booth and grabbed my wrist, pulling me through the crowd like an excited child wanting to show me something she'd found. Her small frame and experience in dealing with the throngs of people in the streets permitted her to weave in and out without effort, but I found myself colliding repeatedly with others as I was dragged along, apologizing as I went. *Way to keep a low profile, Grant. Bumbling your way through the streets apologizing in English. You could at least do it with a Canadian accent.* As a white, unilingual American reporter, I'm fully aware that I'm not going to blend in while traveling. I've accepted this. Instead, I try to downplay it whenever possible. Here's the trick: As a foreigner in a hostile land, don't open your mouth unnecessarily, smile and nod a lot, and don't wear shiny things like expensive wristwatches, shoes, or jewelry. Loud, obtuse travelers with money are almost invariably the first to get kidnapped.

"Hey, Mister American! I give you free gift. Come to my shop!" Like vultures, vendors spotting my complexion and disorientated expression began calling out to me. Aqiylah paid them no attention, continuing to pull my wrist.

An oddly familiar sign for a Starbucks caught my eye as we went along, and I instinctively began moving toward it. Aqiylah stopped, confused, and followed my stare. Playfully tugging me back toward the other side of the street, she yelled, "Those American chains are killing the small local businesses. Come on, I've got a better place in mind."

Turning down a narrow alleyway, she pointed proudly at a pair of folding tables and chairs beneath a hand-painted sign, the word 'Café' trailed by dramatic strokes of Arabic script.

"Here we are."

Reaching for the door, I said, "Let me get that."

"I've got it," she replied, reaching for the handle. For just a second, her palm rested atop my hand. She turned to look at me with a nervous, surprised expression, the reflection of the golden sunrise glittering in her eyes.

"I'm sorry, you go ahead," she said, pulling her hand back as though my skin was boiling water. I almost apologized, but decided against it and walked through the door.

The earthy smell of coffee and tea leaves filled the air as we entered. An arched doorway painted in colorful reds and yellows separated the shop's two small, almost entirely empty rooms. In a corner beneath the building's only window—a narrow aperture rendered opaque by years of dirt sent airborne by street traffic—sat two elderly gentlemen quietly playing a game of backgammon. Sliding into a seat across from me, Aqiylah began playfully drumming the tabletop.

"Is this your first time in Egypt, Grant?"

"I think so."

She giggled. "You think so? How do you not know whether you've been to a country?"

"Well, I started out in Israel, but it's damn hard to know where the Sinai begins and ends."

"Have you been a journalist for a long time?"

"My whole life."

"That must be exciting."

"It certainly can be," I said, recollecting the scattered, alcohol-infused memories of Seoul from a month before, and the all-too-clear ones of the torture I'd endured at the hands of a meth kingpin shortly thereafter in Shanghai. "But it can't compare to all the excitement that's been happening around here, right? I mean this revolt has really escalated in the last few days."

"Uprising, Grant."

"Right. Isn't that what I said?"

"You said revolt. I don't like that word. The Egyptian people are not a band of anarchists ousting a legitimate government, they're rising up against a tyrant and asking for only the essential rights that every human being should have."

"I see. My mistake."

"It's an easy one to make."

A young man approached our table, and Aqiylah smiled at him familiarly.

"Sabi, this is Grant...um...I never caught your last name."

"Cogar. Grant Cogar, pleasure to meet you," I said, shaking his hand.

"He's an American journalist," she said cheerfully.

"Is that right? Well, welcome to the country, Mr. Cogar," he said without the slightest accent. I'm always amazed when traveling how many people speak English. It still makes me feel inadequate and more than a little embarrassed for knowing only smatterings of other languages. From my years of traveling, the most I've learned is how to navigate a bar menu in one of a dozen languages. "Can I get you something to drink?"

"Coffee would be phenomenal."

"Turkish or American?"

"Whatever you'd recommend."

"I'll bring something right out. On the house, of course." He winked at Aqiylah. "And the usual for you?"

"Yes, please."

"Are you hungry? I've got some *basbousa* and *konafa* made, if you'd like."

"I'm sure Grant's hungry." Turning to me, Aqiylah continued, "If you haven't had *basbousa* yet, this is the best place in Cairo to get it. You'll love it."

"Sounds good. What is it?"

"You'll see."

Sabi nodded and turned toward the kitchen.

"So you said your father worked in the States? What did he do?"

"Gun smuggling, mostly," Aqiylah replied casually. I raised an eyebrow and she laughed. "I'm kidding. He was a chemist. He spent a few years as a visiting professor at universities around the country. I went with him once."

"I see. Are you planning to go to school there, too? You've got to be around college age."

She suddenly became solemn.

"I'm eighteen, but I'm not going to school in America. My father died last year in an automobile accident, and I need to stay here and work to help pay for my mother's care. Her health has gotten much worse since my father's death, and she's gone to live with my aunt."

"I'm sorry to hear that, Aqiylah. That's got to be tough for you. I lost my folks when I was too young to even remember them, so I really can't say I know your pain."

"You don't remember them at all?"

"Just shadows, glimpses in my dreams."

"But at least you had your siblings and your extended family to care for you after their passing, right?"

"Nope. I've been on my own since then. Orphanage to orphanage until I was sixteen."

"That must have been a lonely way to go through life. I can't imagine living without my family. I still miss my father so much; I wouldn't have been able to go on if it hadn't been for the support of my relatives."

"It's not so bad. You'd find that the solitude becomes kind of familiar as the years go on," I said, leaning back in my chair. "We're herd animals deep down. The need for social interaction is hardwired right into our physiology—that's tough to just turn off. The trick to overcoming that mentality is to learn to enjoy your own company."

"I don't think I could do it."

Sabi returned with two ceramic cups and set them before us on the table. "Food will be out in a minute."

Raising her cup to touch mine, Aqiylah cracked a smile and said, "Well, here's to the future. May we never be lonelier than we wish."

"Well put."

The coffee, lava hot and black as ebony, went down smoothly. The nagging headache that had been pinballing about my cranium for the past 24 hours vanished as the caffeine entered my system.

"So I suppose we should talk rates."

"I suppose we should."

"I can do 25 bucks a day, and that means you attached to my hip for every step. That'll probably mean long days, and I tend to cover a lot of ground in a short time—I'd expect you to keep up."

She laughed. "You don't need to worry about my keeping up with you, Grant." Pausing and licking her lips thoughtfully, she continued, "I'll translate for 50 American dollars per day, plus meals—starting with this one."

"Fifty?" I shook my head. "Lady, you're way off. I'm curious, who do you think I work for?"

"Is that a rhetorical question?"

"No, it just occurred to me that you don't know who I'm writing for."

"You said you were from Chicago, so I was thinking maybe the *Sun-Times*? Is that the right name for it? I haven't been there in so long; it's hard to remember."

"That's the right name, but the wrong publication. I work for the *Chicago Herald*. You probably *haven't* heard of it. The *Sun-Times* has a readership of, oh, about two million readers. The *Herald*—the publication who'll be paying for your services—has a little less than half a million readers. You may want to adjust your bid accordingly."

"Well come on, barter with me."

I laughed. "Fine. I'll go as high as 35. And I'll throw in an order of that *basbousa* stuff."

Aqiylah raised an eyebrow. "Forty."

Pretending for a moment to be painstakingly mulling the offer over, I finally sighed and said, "Fine. Forty." It would be worth the extra money just to have a beautiful woman to talk to, and, if things went especially well, to keep me warm at night.

"Deal," she said.

I extended my hand. "You drive a hard bargain. You must work in sales."

She smiled and looked away sheepishly, but kept her hand in her lap.

"Ah, right. I'll work on that."

Sabi slid a plate topped with square pastries onto our table as he strolled by. Scooping one into the palm of my hand, I took a bite and said, "You know, you shouldn't give up on your dream to go to school." The *basbousa* had a syrupy sweet taste hinting of coconut. "I mean, I can't say I'd readily go back to college, but it taught me a few things that would have come hard in the real world."

The last words came out in a slur. At first, I thought I was suffering a stroke. Confused, I noticed the edge of my vision blurring, a dizzying sensation overcoming me. Maybe I'd let my blood sugar get too low, or I'd become dehydrated from my bout with food poisoning the night before.

"Aqiylah, would you mind grabbing me a glass of water?" I tried to say. What actually came out was something entirely different, and utterly unintelligible.

The world spun away as I slid from my chair. The last sound I heard was the backgammon players' dice pattering dully, colliding with the game board's cardboard sides as I slipped from consciousness.

7

Days of Rage

Five years before, I'd spent an afternoon lying in an Israeli hospital bed, a burn on my leg—caused by one remarkably well-thrown PLO flashbang grenade—covered in gauze, loaded up with morphine as I read through a week-old Haaretz newspaper. After leisurely filtering through the usual diplomacy and defense-related content about Iran, Hamas, and the successes of the IDF, I turned my attention to the culture section. Featured was a human-interest piece about an elderly Moroccan Jewish pig farmer. The photo showed a sun-wrinkled man standing before his herd, hands folded atop a shovel handle. His clothes were filthy, as was to be expected, and his expression was that of a modest, unassuming farm hand. As I followed the text, I learned the man had survived Nazi internment, the first Arab-Israeli war, and had joined in the action during the Six-Day War before returning to Morocco to take up pig farming. When asked what his key to survival was during all those conflicts, he said something that stuck with me. "I guess I'm just too lucky to die, and too stupid to stay out of trouble."

Too stupid to stay out of trouble. That's me.

I awoke on a dirty mattress thrown on the floor of what I can only readily describe as a dusty, spider web-covered tomb or catacombs, that quotation echoing in my head. I reached to rub my eyes, but my hands stopped short, fastened to the wall with a pair of handcuffs. I've never liked the sensation of being chained up—it's always imparted a sense of helplessness and claustrophobia—but being repeatedly captured and invariably bound with chains of some sort, I'm starting to get used to it.

Illuminated by a bare light bulb suspended from an extension cord stapled to the ceiling, I took in the room's crumbling walls, covered by faded outlines of ancient wall art and engraved hieroglyphs, and a single long, jagged crack in the ceiling revealing the splitting floors of the levels above.

In spite of my attempts to dismiss it, I felt betrayed.

I've always held a naively soft spot in my heart for attractive women, and have been taken advantage of more than once by the gentler sex (I'd like to meet the celibate bastard who coined that phrase) because of that predilection. Hell, in some cases, I'd even invited such treachery by recognizing duplicitous women and pursuing them anyway.

For instance, a couple years ago, I'd stopped at the *Herald's* office to speak with Kailas and grab my paycheck. He introduced me to a smoking-hot, 20-something college student—Mia, I think her name was—who'd just begun interning at the paper during her J-term. I'll just say she had no business in journalism—her God-given talents would have served her far better as a Miami Dolphins cheerleader. Anyway, I'd given her my business card, and that night, got a phone call from her saying she wanted to meet up for dinner to discuss my work—perhaps I'd give her some guidance as she entered the publishing world. Despite the outwardly platonic nature of the meeting, I knew exactly what she was up to.

After a meal of chicken parmigiana and a few rounds of drinks at a classy little joint named 'La Luce' down on West Lake Street, during which she'd taken to rubbing her leg against mine beneath the table and making obvious advances, I'd driven her home and made love to her for hours.

Shamelessly.

The following Monday, she called me on her way to work. She told me she planned to tell Kailas I'd slept with her if I didn't find a way to get her hired on at the *Herald*. I only laughed.

"Promise you won't leave out any of the good parts when you tell him," I'd said before hanging up.

We'd played the same game. That time, I'd won. And I'd won because I understood the price of attraction (and she'd been careless in assuming I was beholden to anyone at the *Herald*—it wasn't as if Kailas was unaware of my affinity for regular female companionship). I'd learned early in life how to protect myself from heartbreak when the inevitable came to pass and I awoke in an empty bed or with my wallet stolen off the nightstand. But this was the first time in many years that I'd been caught so wildly off guard.

With Aqiylah, I'd really thought…well, it doesn't matter what I thought. The fact of the matter was, I should have known better than to trust a stranger no matter how good she was with orphans, how kind she'd been to me, or how much we hit it off. She'd played me, and I was as much ashamed of being manipulated as I was enraged at being imprisoned.

And I had questions. Lots.

Why would anyone want to drug me and take me prisoner? I hadn't had time to do much of anything, let alone piss anyone off—I'd been in the country for less than 24 hours. Was this Colonel Orabi's doing? That wouldn't make much sense; he could have easily had me arrested the minute my plane touched down if this had been his plan. Besides, as far as he knew, I was still soundly sleeping in my hotel room under the watchful eyes of his trusted soldiers. Trusted soldiers who probably needed some supervision to stay on task. How about Aqiylah? What was her role in all this? Was she just the bait, or the mastermind behind my sudden incarceration?

As I contemplated my situation, my eyes wandered to the room's only door. It stood a foot ajar, and through the gap, I spotted something I'd recognize anywhere—a nearly naked woman.

Aqiylah.

She'd removed her head cover, revealing straight brown hair that fell past the shoulder—so dark it appeared black in this light. She'd shed her working clothes and had begun slowly padding a moist washcloth against her bare arms and along her toned abdomen. She made me jump in anticipation as she slid her bra straps from her shoulders and wiped the sweat from her collar. She was angelic in her elegance, a testament to the grace of the female form. Athletic and slender, her olive-skinned body glowed in the low light as her large, intelligent, peridot-colored eyes shined like gemstones. Her full breasts and shapely legs worked the way a syringe filled with amphetamines and plunged through my sternum would—my heart raced wildly.

Though my eyes were fixed firmly to her flawless form, I couldn't help but think how quickly and brutally I'd be put to death if anyone knew I'd seen Aqiylah like this. In this part of the world, anything but the most modest attire garnered critical shouts from the conservative public. Have a young, unmarried woman inadvertently expose herself to an American tourist? That'd be met with a little more hostility.

Something tickled my leg, pulling my eyes away from the spectacle.

Craning my neck, my stomach lurched as I discovered a large, black- and orange-colored scorpion making its way toward my groin, its stinger bouncing as it moved.

Looking back at Aqiylah as she continued to clean herself, I fought a brief internal battle between my wish to see more of her and my fear of large, poisonous arachnids in close proximity to my manhood.

Biting my lip as I glanced at the creature, I whimpered, "Aqiylah!"

She disappeared from view momentarily, likely redressing. Entering the room, she knelt down by the mattress. She'd thrown on a sleeveless tee shirt and a pair of shorts, to my disappointment.

"How are you feeling?"

"I'd feel a whole lot better if you'd get that fucking thing off of my leg," I said, trying to stay still but wanting very much to thrash violently.

"Oh," she said nonchalantly, grabbing the scorpion by its stinger and tossing it toward a far wall. "How's that?"

"Good," I said, relieved and more than a little impressed by her audacity. "But I'd feel even better if you'd unchain me and tell me why you brought me here."

"I can't, sorry."

"You drugged me, didn't you?"

"Mandrake bark—an ancient sleep aid. Not poppy, nor mandrake, nor all the drowsy syrups of the world shall ever medicine thee to that sweet sleep which thou owedst yesterday," she recited proudly.

"That's beautiful—you write that just for this occasion?"

"Shakespeare's *Othello*. I'm sorry for having to do this, but it's for your own safety. You were being followed by Colonel Orabi's men."

"That boy in the marketplace, he told you," I said, flashing back to the moment the eldest child leaned in and whispered in her ear. "Then, when you led me to the coffee shop, the server asked you if you wanted *basbousa* or *konafa*. That was the indicator question—friend or foe. You asked for the *basbousa*, and he poisoned my coffee."

"Poisoned is a strong word. Drugged sounds a little better. Either way, I'm sorry."

"You're sorry? You could have just told me that I was being followed and asked me to come with you," I said. "I didn't even know. I thought I'd lost the guards at the hotel."

"It's hard to know who to trust sometimes. We weren't sure if you were just unaware of the guards, or if you were working on behalf of the government."

"Have you figured it out yet?"

"I've got a pretty good idea, but we didn't want to take any chances."

"Good. Well now you can cut me loose. I told you the truth before; I work for the *Chicago Herald*. I'm not taking sides here, I just want to get at the truth and do my job."

"When the others get here, we'll let you go. I can't be the one to do it." Aqiylah gently moved her hand against my forehead, her fingers softly brushing my temple. "You seem to be fine."

"Why wouldn't I be?"

Clearing her throat, she looked at me sheepishly, "Mandrake can be poisonous, and you drank your coffee very quickly. Very American."

"Yeah, well you dress very American, for an Egyptian woman."

Suddenly defensive, she leaned back and crossed her arms.

"I shouldn't have to worry about the way I dress, Grant. I'm a free woman, and I'm entitled to feel attractive, to not feel ashamed of my body. Society uses the guise of modesty to further suppress the liberty of women. If I wasn't so sure I'd be accosted, I'd dress this way when I go out, too."

"Aqiylah, what are you doing?" A young man entered the room and grabbed her shoulder. I recognized him as the same gentleman who had brought our drinks at the coffee shop a few hours before. Since I hadn't been given the opportunity to pay him for our drinks and his service, I felt I owed him something—like a swift punch in the mouth.

In his late 20s, he stood about six feet tall and wore a pair of clean blue jeans and a striped polo shirt. With dark hair cut short and a clean-shaven face—apart from a small patch of facial hair beneath his bottom lip— he could have easily passed for a European tourist.

"Don't speak to him. Wait until the others get here."

He looked nervous, which made me nervous.

"Sabi, calm down. He's on our side."

I wondered what his relationship to Aqiylah was.

"On our side?" he scoffed. "He's an American journalist—he couldn't be further from it." Lowering his voice, he continued, "In fact, Rashid says that this man dined with Colonel Orabi last night. You thought he was being followed by the colonel's men, but he was being protected by them."

Aqiylah looked at me, her eyes afire. "Is this true?"

I let my head fall to the mattress. My skull throbbed, and I felt sapped of all the energy needed to explain myself.

Suddenly noticing how Aqiylah was dressed, Sabi's face grew red, his eyes wide and his jaw clenched.

"You're going to wear clothes like this with Kek and his men coming? You know how the Brotherhood views such attire."

"I didn't know they were coming." Looking to the floor angrily, Aqiylah whispered, "Besides, the Brotherhood is wrong."

Sabi looked as though he was on the verge of a rage-filled outburst. Then, suddenly regaining his composure, his features softened and he touched her shoulder. "I know, Aqiylah. But we must take one step at a time. Democracy first." His reaction told me that he was a man fighting to sequester a naturally volatile temper. Was he trying to play nice to win over Aqiylah? I suddenly felt an urge to compete for her attention.

"And what does democracy represent? Freedom? Oh, but only for men?" She stomped her foot against the packed-dirt floor and stormed out of the room.

Pointing a finger at me threateningly, Sabi turned and followed her.

Calling after them, I shouted, "Okay…so, I guess I'll just wait here?"

8

A Paid Killer

"Got a whale of a tale to tell ya, lads, a whale of a tale or toohoo," I bellowed for the fiftieth time that hour. Bored, thirsty, and desperately needing to take a piss, I was beginning to worry my captors had forgotten about me entirely or had left the premises.

"About the flappin' fish and the girls I've loved, on nights like this with the moon above…"

An hour before, I'd taken to singing the most obnoxious, repetitive songs I knew in hopes I'd at least get them to come yell at me and possibly allow me to relieve myself somewhere other than my pants.

"A whale of a tale and it's all true, I swear by my tattoo."

Though it was probably a comfortable 80 degrees outside, the glowing sun now completely covered the crack in the roof and cast its rays upon me relentlessly. My face and neck burned as sweat trickled into my eyes and down the bridge of my nose.

Just as I was deciding whether to do another verse of "100 Bottles of Beer on the Wall" or switch to "The Song that Never Ends", I heard footsteps on the other side of the doorway. Aqiylah swung open the room's faded blue-painted door and walked briskly toward me. She'd once again donned her working clothes and *hijab*.

"What'd you think of my singing?"

"Intolerable," she said.

"That's disheartening, I was planning on taking it on the road."

"Kek is on his way. Perhaps you can sing to him."

"Sure. Who?"

"Kek. He's a paid killer. The Brotherhood uses him to remove their most stubborn competition and those critical of the party. You must have really angered someone—Sabi says they only use him under the most dire circumstances."

Ignoring the new information, I asked, "You suppose I could get a drink of water or something?" What I really wanted was a cold beer and ticket back to Seoul or Chicago.

Looking at me doubtfully, she reluctantly left the room and returned with a canteen. Unscrewing its cap, she held the back of my head and tipped it toward my mouth. Despite her detached attitude, her touch was gentle.

"He won't kill you straightaway, though. He enjoys torturing his victims."

After taking a long drink, I said quietly, "As long as he's willing to sing high harmony, I think we'll get along alright."

Looking dispassionately at the wall, she said hollowly, "You don't realize what you're up against. But you deserve what you get for aligning yourself with the president's pawn, Colonel Orabi."

In one quick motion, I grabbed Aqiylah's wrist—my handcuff's chain snapping taught against the steel anchor in the wall, the canteen falling from her hand and clattering to the floor. I pulled her toward me until her face was inches from mine. Her breath smelled sweet and a little tart, like raspberries.

"I deserve what I get? I've gotten about all I can handle, girlie, and I *just* set foot in your goddamn country. I don't know why you drugged me, I don't know why you've kept me tied up all morning, and I don't know why you think I'm here to support the Egyptian government. You're familiar with the first amendment of the U.S. Constitution? That part about protecting the freedom of speech? That's my bread and butter—my livelihood. You don't think I would fight and die to keep that right the way you would to get it?"

The hardness in her eyes disappeared instantly, replaced, instead, with tears.

"Let go of my wrist."

I did. She retreated to a corner of the room and rubbed her arm. I hadn't grabbed her hard enough to hurt her.

After a moment, she said, "How do I know you aren't working for the government?"

"You'll have to take my word for it and trust me." I struggled with saying that last part—I was still a long way off from trusting *her*. In fact, I was still angry enough at my incarceration and poor treatment that I didn't much care if she believed me or not. I just wanted out of this cave. But in order to accomplish that, I would need her help, and as I'd learned during my days as an embedded journalist, the most hostile territory is that in which you have no allies.

"I don't trust you or anyone," she said, sounding an awful lot like a teenager at war with the world.

"That seems extreme," I said, my voice softening.

"No, you know what's extreme, Grant? Imprisoning a fifty-year-old man for civil disobedience, beating him to death, and then telling his family he died in a car wreck."

"Your father," I said stupidly, staring at the ceiling and wishing I'd been born mute.

"I was helpless to stop it," she choked as she broke down sobbing. "The policemen laughed when they told us. That's how obvious it was they were lying."

Over the years, I'd heard whispers from other reporters about the corruption within the Egyptian government and the underhanded means by which they'd eliminate those who might subvert their plans. For as long as I'd been in the business, Egypt had been a red zone for reporters for that very reason—if you were careless and started asking the wrong people the right questions, you could easily end up "disappeared." It had never meant anything to me beyond my own self-preservation. But the pain I saw in Aqiylah's eyes when she mentioned her father reminded me that not everyone had the luxury of avoiding this place. To some, this was home. This was life.

A door slammed a floor above us followed by the dull trampling of a man's footsteps.

"I'm sorry," I said, genuinely meaning each word. I was beginning to understand Aqiylah's obsessive mistrust of all things linked to the government, and felt as though her suspicion—though inconvenient as hell for me—may not have been as baseless as I'd originally believed.

"No, you're not. You don't understand what I've had to go through to get here; the sacrifices my family and I have made," she said. Collecting herself with a deep breath, she balled her hands into fists and took on a resolute expression. "This government has been broken for years, and to fix it, to have our voices heard without fear of soldiers kicking in our doors in the night, being beaten and interrogated, we need to ally ourselves with anyone who might help us. Right now, the Muslim Brotherhood is the best chance we've got to oust the president and finally have democratic elections. But they're Islamic fundamentalists with their own agenda, and women will never be completely free or equal under their rule, either. I have to choose the lesser of the two evils, knowing that such a decision is a wrong one, too."

I was suddenly filled with the desire to comfort her. Yep, just like that: A pretty girl cries, and the fury of Cogar is promptly extinguished. Just another display of that naïve soft spot I'd mentioned before. It'll probably get me killed someday.

Sabi burst into the room abruptly, and Aqiylah hastily wiped at her cheeks with the back of her hand as she hid her face.

"Quickly, they're here."

Heavy, echoing footfalls of two men sounded down the hall as they made their way into the room. The larger of the two wore a robe—a hood pulled over his head. The other, a short, clean-shaven man with an emaciated build, wore a plain black tee shirt and military issued cargo pants—the dark clothes accentuating his pale complexion. He walked a few steps behind his larger companion.

"*As-salamu alaykum.*"

Sabi and Aqiylah responded simultaneously, "*Wa alaykum as-salam.*"

Turning toward me, the robed man lifted his hood, revealing a broad, toad-like face topped with curly black hair fading to silver. The deep wrinkles of his forehead appeared calloused and darkened—likely the sign of years spent touching it to carpet during prayer. He smelled like a sweaty onion.

"I'm sure you don't know who I am or why I'm here, Mr. Cogar, so allow me to introduce myself. My name is Kazemde El-Shafik, Secretary General of the

Muslim Brotherhood's Freedom and Justice Party." He spoke with a thick accent, and I struggled to fully grasp what the big man was saying.

"Pleasure. You'll understand if I don't get up," I said, tugging at my restraints just enough to make the chain rattle.

"Young man, this is no time for sarcasm. You are in a great deal of danger," he said, looking sideways at the figure beside him. Though of a slighter build than Shafik and approximately the same age, the man possessed a more unsettling demeanor. A black patch covered only some of the gaping wound that had apparently claimed his eye. A scar above his lip had tightened the skin into a permanent grimace, revealing a mouth full of yellow, broken teeth. This, I thought, must be Kek. "Many in my party are calling for your expulsion from our country. Others would rather see you killed and made an example of. You see, they think that you and the other American reporters are working for your government, and are attempting to slander our name."

"And why would we do a thing like that?"

The big man chuckled. "Your government and ours, they are like this," he said, crossing his arms and locking his hands together. "For years, the United States sends billions of dollars to Egypt. And who runs Egypt? Mubarak and his army. They would do anything to keep Islam from regaining power here. Can you blame our people for looking at Americans skeptically?"

"If it means my execution, then yes, I can blame them. I haven't touched pen to paper since I've been here. And you're accusing me of conspiring against your cause?"

The big man laughed heartily, his voice deep and soothing in its joviality.

"Personally, I don't believe that's the case. I think having reporters like you here will let the world know of our plight. Our struggle is a right and just one, *mash'allah*. We have nothing to be ashamed of. We also have no intention to harm you, Mr. Cogar. In fact, we brought you here out of concern for your wellbeing. President Mubarak has made it clear in recent days that not only are revolutionaries in danger, journalists are targets, too. He believes you are at the root of the protests. Communication is dangerous to a dictator, as I'm sure you know."

I said nothing. The outwardly equitable nature of every party who had successfully kept me from getting any work done since my arrival was beginning to piss me off.

If they were all on my side, why did I feel as though I couldn't trust anyone?

"Unfortunately, my friend, you are caught in the middle of a war you know very little about."

"It's pretty hard to learn anything about it when no one will let me off the leash."

"You don't understand. Mr. Cogar, this is for your own health."

That made me laugh. I'd stopped being concerned about my health around the time I turned thirteen. A man doesn't make much of a living as a war journalist if he's spending all his time hiding from things that might shorten his lifespan.

"Right. Well, I like to keep things exciting," I said. "I get bored so easily these days, you know?"

Shafik nodded slowly, glancing at Kek out of the corner of his eye. The smaller man was a statue, standing perfectly still as he looked at me with a stare so empty I wondered if he'd died standing upright.

"Someone want to check that guy's pulse? He doesn't look so good," I said, motioning toward Shafik's companion with my head.

Ignoring me, Shafik asked, "Did you enjoy your meal with Colonel Orabi?"

"Meh, it was so-so. The lamb was a little rare for my tastes."

Sabi rushed toward me, hands held open, ready to strangle. Aqiylah slipped between the two of us and grabbed Sabi's shoulders.

"You see?" Sabi yelled. "He is a sympathizer. He cannot be allowed to stay."

"Wow, and you're supposed to be the spear point for democracy in Egypt," I scoffed. "But you're ready to silence anyone who dines with your opposition? Sounds an awful lot like fascism. How does that one roll off the tongue, asshole?"

"We're not fascist, Mr. Cogar, but we are certainly cautious," Shafik said. "I'm afraid Sabi is correct; we'll need you to leave the country immediately. I'll send my guards along with you to retrieve your bags from the hotel. Then, I must insist that you go directly to the airport. We will welcome you back to this country with open arms when we have accomplished our goals."

"Somehow I doubt that."

"Please, release Mr. Cogar from his shackles," Shafik said, waving at Sabi.

A raspy voice, almost inhuman, hissed from Kek's mouth, "But Kazemde, what if he escape? Allow me kill him and trouble us no more." Aqiylah's description of the man had clearly not been too far off. He certainly was hostile. Must have caught his mom in bed with a reporter as a child.

Shafik turned to the shorter man and said, "You Syrians—so eager to shed blood. There is a time and a place for violence; this is not it." Looking at Sabi, he continued, "I'm afraid I must leave. The protests in Tahrir Square are escalating, and I must stay close to our brothers. Today could be our day of victory." Pulling his hood over his head, he turned to leave, Kek following reluctantly. Stopping in the hallway, Shafik spoke over his shoulder, "Mr. Cogar, you will be followed until your plane leaves the tarmac. Entertain no illusions of escape."

9

City of the Dead

"I really need to pee, guys," I pleaded with two of Shafik's lackeys as they hustled me outside. "I've been holding it for hours." Holding my knees together, I made a pained face to convey my meaning.

The larger of the two men, a bearded behemoth cloaked in a loose fitting, cream-colored *galabiya*—a traditional collarless robe—reluctantly conceded. Shoving me toward a dark corner of the building's entryway, he followed a few steps behind. A red velveteen *tarbush* sat atop his head, complete with a dangling tassel I wanted to bat around like a cat.

Unzipping my fly, I said, "You planning on holding it for me, too? How about a little privacy, pork chop?"

He ignored me, hovering a few feet away as his partner stood in the doorway.

"You guys seem to have an unusual fascination with male genitalia. Tired of ogling livestock?" I asked over my shoulder knowing they couldn't understand me.

When I'd finished, he barely gave me time to zip my pants before dragging me toward a road-worn taxi outside, opening the back door, and hurling me inside. My guards entered and sat on either side of me. Aqiylah and Sabi followed a few minutes later, the latter pulling the keys from his pocket and dropping casually into the driver's seat.

Blinking my eyes at the harsh sunlight, I leaned away from the shoulder of the larger guard on my right. "When did you bathe last, dude? No judgments here, just curious."

He responded with a snarl, his breath hot and reeking of chewing tobacco and putrefaction.

"Down, boy." Leaning toward the front seat, I asked, "So where were we, exactly?"

The car slowly rolled amidst a large crowd in the dusty street.

"*El'arafa*," Sabi said blankly from the driver's seat as he pulled a pack of smokes from his shirt pocket, and, steering with his knee, reached for the car's cigarette lighter.

"City of the Dead—the Cairo Necropolis. Thousands live here in family tombs because they can't afford to live elsewhere or can't find adequate housing," Aqiylah explained. On a rooftop nearby, an elderly woman slapped a large, dusty rug against the building's wall and cast us a mostly-toothless smile as we drove by. "Most Cairenes find it distasteful to live here or are intimidated by its reputation as a cemetery, but it's become a really close-knit community. It's the ideal place to begin our work forming a democracy: a city within, but still apart from, Cairo," Aqiylah said loftily, swirling her finger in the thick layer of dust resting on the car's dashboard.

"Start small, right?" I asked.

She laughed.

"If you consider five million people small, then yes."

"And I take it living in tombs must be frowned upon by the Egyptian government?"

"It's illegal, yes. And like I said, much of Cairo looks down upon those who live here. Some consider it dishonorable—turning a sacred site into a homestead, hanging laundry from gravestones, you know. But it's not as though they're given much of a choice."

The vehicle crept forward, coming to a complete stop as a particularly large crowd migrated toward a man standing in the bed of a pickup truck.

"Open-air preacher?" I joked.

"Hotel worker," Aqiylah replied. "The tourist trade produces an enormous amount of waste that these people desperately need. Fruit that's gone brown, cheese and bread that have begun to mold, these things can't be served to Americans and Europeans, but they mean the difference between starvation and survival out here. It's either this or stand in line for hours just to buy a loaf of cheap, government-subsidized bread."

Sabi, irritated by the wait, took to bumping the car's horn and rolling down his window to shout and wave the pedestrians away from the vehicle's front bumper. His voice was lost among the din. The brotherhood's guards stepped out of the car and began clearing a path for Sabi to drive through. Spotting my opportunity, I leaned forward in my seat, slid aside Aqiylah's *hijab* and kissed her ear tenderly, whispering, "I've gotta run; good luck with your revolt," before leaping from the car and dashing into the crowd.

Suddenly realizing what I'd done, Sabi and Aqiylah slipped out of their seatbelts and began their pursuit, shouting and gesturing wildly at the two guards and pointing in my direction.

Staying low and slipping through the crowd, I ducked into an alleyway and began scaling the wall of an adobe building, my fingers scraping for a handhold as I heaved myself upwards and away from my captors.

The smaller of the two guards—clearly a nimble man—closed the distance quickly, bowling over unprepared onlookers and quickly sidestepping those too large to knock over. Leaping from the ground, he managed to wrap a hand around my ankle, fingertips digging into my skin, just as I secured a hold on a wood joist protruding from the building's side. Feeling myself pulled down, I began desperately scraping at the heel of my leather loafer with my free foot. My pursuer fell to the dirt heavily with my footwear in hand. Once I'd climbed up, I slipped off my remaining shoe and began leaping from one rooftop to the next, the sun-dried boards beneath my feet bending under my weight and puffing clouds of dust into the air as they rebounded. *Fools*, I thought, *I'm Grant Cogar, master escape artist. No mortal bonds can hold me.*

Like a stallion turned loose into open pasture, I felt spurred on by waves of adrenaline coursing through my veins as I raced through the dry desert air. But upon reaching the next rooftop, I slid to an abrupt stop—face to face with Aqiylah.

Holy shit, she's quick.

In her right hand, pointed at my chest, she held a 9mm Helwan pistol. An outdated weapon originally made for the Egyptian army, I knew from my time in Iraq that most of these Beretta clones had been so poorly manufactured, they didn't even make good war prizes.

"You sure that thing's going to go off?" I asked boldly. Though I knew the weapon wasn't a quality one, that didn't change the fact that it only needed to work once, and I would be on my way to an agonizing death on a rooftop, in the middle of the desert, without shoes or a friend in sight.

Ignoring me, she said, "It's not a revolt, Grant. It's an uprising."

"What?" I asked, confused.

"As you were jumping out of the car, you said 'good luck with the revolt'. I told you before; it's not a revolt. It's an uprising. Now get back in the car."

"Let me go, Aqiylah. I've done nothing to you, or the Muslim Brotherhood, or anyone else. I just wanted to do my job and take you out for coffee. I didn't think that was asking too much." I continued to eye the handgun's blued steel, tracing an imaginary line from the muzzle to my chest.

"You know I can't let you go. I like you, Grant, I really do, and I do believe you when you say you aren't working against us. But I have loyalties that run much deeper than our friendship. Please, I don't want to shoot you, but so help me, if you take one more step, I'll drop you where you stand." Her *hijab* had slipped from her head to her neck during the pursuit, and her dark hair glowed in the mid-morning sunlight, tousled by the breeze.

Doubting that she'd shoot me but not wanting to be wrong, I stepped toward her cautiously.

"Fine. We'll do it your way. But we walk back together, like friends."

Lowering her weapon slightly, her eyes pleading, she said, "Grant, I *am* sorry about this."

"Yeah, me too," I sighed as I stepped past her. In no hurry to get back in the car, I asked, "How'd you get up here so quickly?"

"Same way you did," she said, stepping to my side as I peered over the edge of the roof. "I climbed. As much as you wanted to escape, I wanted to catch you."

I smiled and looked at her. "Because you liked my kiss so much you just had to have another?"

She laughed and raised her eyebrow, "Your breath smells terrible, and if that was the best kiss you can muster, I think I could do better."

"Hey, you guys didn't exactly take great care of me back there. No mint on my pillow, no complimentary toothpaste…"

"I'll be sure to pass your concerns on to management," she kidded, bumping me with her shoulder playfully. I was finding it difficult to stay angry with this girl.

Taking a deep breath, I looked at her solemnly. "Aqiylah, you understand that I'm sticking around until this story is done, right? I mean, you guys can take me back to my hotel, but I didn't come halfway around the globe to go home empty-handed."

"I hope you get what you're looking for, Grant. I just can't let you escape on my watch, or it would look suspicious to the Brotherhood. We need their support right now."

"I know you've got to look out for your interests. But I'm going to look out for mine, too."

She nodded and looked away. "We should get back. Glancing at her feet, she tapped a piece of gravel with the toe of her tennis shoe, chewed her lip, and said quietly, "And thanks, Grant."

"For what?"

"For understanding my predicament. I mean, if you had been anyone else, this could have ended very differently. I really don't like the idea of shooting anyone."

"And?" I probed.

"God, you're conceited! Fine. For the kiss, too, I guess," she said, her cheeks blushing as she looked up with a smirk.

We climbed down and walked back to the car. When Sabi saw us approach, he rushed me—grabbing my shirt collar with his left hand and slapping me in the face with the open palm of his right. More surprised than injured from the blow, I chuckled. "Really? Slapping? Tell me that's not the best you've got, princess."

Squeezing his hand into a balled fist, Sabi prepared to strike me again. Aqiylah nudged between us, arms crossed.

"You hit him again, Sabi, and next time I'll *help* him escape."

"There'll be no next time," Sabi growled, pointing toward the car's back seat. "Get in the car and stay in there."

The meaty hand of the Brotherhood's trained Sasquatch gripped the back of my neck, and I was shoved inside with something less than tender finesse.

"Wait!" I exclaimed. "I need my shoes."

"What? What'd you do with your shoes?" Aqiylah asked, confused.

"He took one of them," I said, pointing a finger menacingly at the shorter guard. "Yeah, don't think I don't know it was you, you footwear-stealing bastard."

"Tough," Sabi said. "We're taking you back to your hotel, you can get new shoes there."

Leaning back in my seat dejectedly, I stared off into the distant horizon for a moment before asking, "How far are the pyramids of Giza from here?"

"You never shut up, do you?" Sabi growled.

"Simple question. If you don't know, you can just say so. There's no shame in that. People back in Chi-Town ask me for directions all the time and I can't always help them."

"They're not far, Grant," Aqiylah said. "Fifteen minutes north of here, give or take."

"We have time for a camel ride? I've always wanted to have my photo taken with me riding a camel in front of the pyramids. Might be difficult to explain why I don't have my shoes on in the photo when I'm showing my vacation slides, but…"

Reaching below his seat, Sabi withdrew a folded newspaper and, reaching over his shoulder, hurled it at my chest.

"Shut up, you worthless American pig."

Unshaken, I unfolded the paper and swung a leg over my knee. "You're done with this, then?"

****

We spent the remainder of the half-hour ride in silence as I tried to catch Aqiylah's eye in the rearview mirror. As we pulled to a stop outside the Conrad Cairo, I exited following the Brotherhood's men, the asphalt hot on my feet, and walked around to the passenger side, knocking on Aqiylah's window. She rolled it down.

"Abduction and the death threats aside, it was a pleasure getting to meet you, Aqiylah," I said, offering her my hand. "Maybe next time—" Before I could finish my sentence or even fully reclaim my hand from inside the car, Sabi jammed his foot on the gas pedal and whipped back into the street.

"I'm beginning to think that guy doesn't like me," I said to my chaperones.

Sabi's conduct around Aqiylah—violently protective of her and aggressive toward me—seemed a pretty clear indication that he was entertaining some love interest for the girl. Understandable, really. I tend to fall for strong-willed, strong-bodied women, too.

"Oh well. Who's up for hitting the pool?"

As I headed toward the entrance, I suddenly stopped and turned on my heel, snapping my fingers playfully.

"It just occurred to me: You boys are card-carrying members of the Muslim Brotherhood, and a certain Colonel Saif al-Orabi—yeah, I figured you've heard of him—went through the trouble of posting a few of his soldiers on guard duty right outside that door." Pointing toward the two uniformed men at the entrance, I waved at them and continued, "See 'em? You boys don't get along well with authority, do you? Maybe it'd be best if you waited in the parking lot, huh?"

The two men looked at each other, their expressions deadpan. Turning around, I yelled over my shoulder, "If you're good, I might sneak you fellas some lunch." Passing the colonel's guards, I grinned as they looked at me curiously over their cigarettes.

Upon entering the hotel, I looked around and took a deep breath—suddenly aware of how much cleaner the air was indoors. Strolling toward the hotel's lounge, I picked up a week-old copy of the Egypt Independent and began paging through it. Though it did give me a small sense of relief to know that the majority of my competition—cowards, the lot of them—were probably still wearing their pajamas and waiting in their rooms for permission to go outside, I couldn't shake the feeling that my window of opportunity to gather sources and information for my article was passing by. My experiences with the colonel and Aqiylah had been colorful, and had painted a clear picture of two very different perspectives on the same conflict, but I needed some firsthand exposure to the protests to really feel confident as I sat down to write. But with the colonel's troops and the Brotherhood's guards waiting for me outside, I'd have to be more creative than I'd been that morning in order to regain my sovereignty.

The answer to my problems approached me from the elevator. Marching toward me determinedly, bags in hand, Perry called out, "Cogar? Look, I know we've never seen see eye-to-eye...wait. Where are your shoes?"

Looking down at my dirt-covered feet, I replied, "I'm preparing for a coming of age ritual in which I must walk across burning coals wearing only a pair of socks. Why do you ask?"

Shaking his head in confusion, he continued, "Look, Cogar, I'm warning you—these guys aren't messing around. They made it pretty clear if we don't leave the country, we're going to end up sleeping with the pharaohs."

"Who are you talking about?"

"The revolutionaries. Didn't they threaten you, too?"

"Revolutionaries?" It suddenly dawned on me who Perry was talking about. *Well at least the Brotherhood is fair in their threats—I'd hate to be the only one they ordered out of the country.* "You should go, then, Perry," I said mockingly. "It *is* pretty scary here." I folded my newspaper and tossed it on a nearby table. "Am I too late for the continental breakfast?"

Suddenly becoming indignant, Perry dropped his bags to the carpet.

"I'm not afraid, it just seems foolish to stay here. I don't take death threats lightly, Cogar."

"I'm not in your way, am I?" I asked, stepping to the side. "If you want to run home and miss out on your story, be my guest. Some of us still subscribe to the belief that we're reporters, and we're here to do a job—not work on our tan."

From the street, the parade-like sound of thousands of footfalls and shouts made its way into the hotel lobby. Eager to direct the conversation away from his shortcomings, Perry said, "Sounds like the protests are picking up again."

"You feel like joining in?" I asked tauntingly.

"No, but even if I did, how would we get past the revolutionaries? They said they'd be watching me."

"Give me your hand."

"What? No."

"Do you want to escape from here or not?"

"Not really…"

Grabbing his wrist, I hauled him toward a nearby wall.

"You, Perry Rothko, have the power to change the course of our fate with just this one hand," I said, lifting his arm in front of him. He continued to pull away uncomfortably. "You wanted to earn my trust, right? Be buddies?" I asked.

"Well, yeah."

"Then you have to trust me, first."

Relaxing slightly, he nodded. "Okay, fine."

Slamming his hand down against the emergency fire alarm, I grinned as sirens sounded throughout the building.

"After you." I gestured toward the growing crowd of guests heading toward the exits.

Perry's expression was torn between betrayal, anger, and fear. "So help me, Cogar, if this comes back on me, I'm telling them you did it."

"That's fine. I'll just tell them you work for the Defense Intelligence Agency."

"I don't even know what that is."

"Good point. They'd never believe me. Just look at you—you'd never pass for a spy."

Reaching into his bags before stuffing them behind a chair in the corner, Perry withdrew a very nice SLR digital camera, slipping its strap around his neck, and a tablet computer.

"Nice toys."

"Only the best. That's how I separate myself from the wannabes."

I chuckled. Like a bad golfer who thinks buying more expensive clubs will help shave a few strokes off his game, Perry was laughably mistaken in thinking nicer equipment would do anything to help his writing. Considering how many times I'd had my phone, camera, computer, and voice recorder stolen, confiscated, or destroyed, I now only carry that which I can readily replace or live without. Perry would find that out eventually. If he ever took risks, that is.

Following the crowd down the hotel steps and into the streets, Colonel Orabi's guards and the Brotherhood's men overwhelmed by the sudden exodus, we stepped away and joined the growing throng as they marched away from the hotel and toward Tahrir Square.

I grinned. Over the years, I've found that almost any time a dictator or military leader is threatened with exposure of their crimes and tries to strong-arm civilians or reporters into silence or cooperation, he's certain to fail. This was a case in point—despite their best efforts to contain me and keep me quiet, both the Muslim Brotherhood and Colonel Orabi could now enjoy the sensation of me slipping through their fingers. Their aggressive efforts to keep me from the truth had only driven me on—piranha-like, as Orabi had said— in search of what they were trying so hard to hide. Like a kid seeking out hidden Easter candy, their lack of transparency and attempts to throw me off the trail were just part of the game, and had only intrigued me further. No threat of death or injury has ever successfully forced me to turn that off.

As I scanned the crowd, I noticed beside us a middle-aged man clad in a tweed jacket, slacks, and a pair of spectacles. He strolled along with a quiet determination, his hands behind his back, one wrapped around the wrist of the other. I hoped his scholarly appearance was a reflection of his language skills.

Dodging around the people walking between us, I sidled up to the man, pulled the pen and small notepad from my pocket, and shouted, "Excuse me, but do you mind if I ask you a few questions? I'm a journalist with the *Chicago Herald*."

Turning to look at me over his wire-rimmed bifocals, he smiled and answered, "Chicago? I love Chicago. I once spent a summer near Evanston. So beautiful by the water."

Bullseye, Cogar. You've still got the gift: You know a good source when you see one.

"It certainly is, Mister..."

"Ahmed Ghoneim, professor of anthropology at Sinai University. And you are?"

"Grant Cogar. Pleasure." I offered him my hand, but before he could shake it, a small crowd of young men shoving their way toward the front of the horde abruptly knocked me to the pavement.

"You here on vacation, then, I take it?" Ghoneim asked jokingly as he helped me to my feet.

"What can I say? I got a wicked-good deal on airline fare," I replied, dusting off my slacks and fingering the new tear in my suit jacket.

"Joking aside, you are very blessed to be here right now," Ghoneim said. "These are the days when the true Egypt shines through. Our people have been repressed, and now we are banding together as a shining example of humanity to break these shackles."

"Is that what brings you here, Ahmed? To fight against repression?" I asked, flipping through the pages of my notepad in search of a clean one void of scribbles, sketches I'd made during boring press conferences, and nearly illegible notes I'd taken during interviews. I do that intentionally: writing in shorthand and abbreviations that make a doctor's handwriting look as though it'd been done by a calligrapher. That way, if my notes get confiscated or fall into the wrong hands, they're worthless and can't be used to incriminate me.

"Yes, but mostly I am here for my good friend, Khaled. The police beat him to death in Alexandria last year. I owe it to him to fight back against such brutality and disdain for human life, to persevere and help my people regain their freedom."

"What will it take to make that happen? I mean, should you get Mubarak to step down, will that be enough?"

Blinking away the low-hanging smoke from a burning car nearby, Ghoneim pulled the glasses from his head and wiped the lenses against his shirt. "For decades, as long as I can remember, the military has controlled every aspect of our lives. Our leaders—Mubarak included—have always been military leaders. They control the economy and make the laws. As long as this continues, we will not be free. I don't know if removing the president from power will be enough—it probably isn't—but it's a start all the same."

"Do you think this movement will be successful?"

He turned to me and gave me a knowing smile as he placed his glasses back in place. "Of course I do, with all my heart." Sweeping a hand toward the throngs around us, he continued, "Mubarak has always proudly exercised his power while hiding behind the power of his army. But now, with the entire nation coming down upon him and his soldiers leaving his side for our cause, we have proven to him, and to the world, that now is the time for a new Egypt."

A stone the size of a fist sailed by my head toward a distant army cordon—rows of black-clad soldiers holding riot shields edge to edge. In response to the stones and glass bottles being hurled at them, the government forces began firing 40-millimeter C2 gas canisters from behind the barricade.

Like a rock concert crowd singing a chorus, the protestors cried in unison, "*Irhal! Irhal!*"

"Ahmed, what are they yelling?" I found myself shouting directly into his ear to be heard above the uproar.

"*Irhal.* It means leave! They are speaking to the president."

Overspray from fire hoses fell like rain on our shoulders as waves of the stinging gas rolled over us in a dense fog. Striving to see through the increasingly heavy smoke and jostling crowd, I decided I needed a better vantage point.

I've found that, even with the aid of modern technology, battlefield reporting hasn't changed much over the centuries. The reporter needs to be amidst the conflict to portray the battle realistically in his writing, but the fog of war has a singular way of dropping a veil of confusion over all those involved in the conflict, reducing the reporter's scope. In other words, if he's on the ground, he knows what the soldiers are experiencing, but doesn't have the full view of the battlefield the way he would from an aircraft overhead. But if one can find a way to experience both perspectives, they have all the ingredients for an accurate, gripping article. Now I just had to find myself an airplane.

Or a flagpole.

Eyeing the steel beam 20 feet away and following its line into the smoke-laden sky, I slapped Ahmed on the back and yelled, "Good luck."

He smiled, apparently unfazed by the increasing violence around him. "You too, Mr. Cogar. I'll keep an eye out for your article."

I hadn't taken two steps away from the professor before a man with a bulky television camera on his shoulder grabbed me. His features blurred as my eyes began to burn from the wafting tear gas.

"You speak English? Ennnglisshhh?" he shouted at me.

"Yeah, though yours needs some work."

Sighing with relief, the man yelled, "You a journalist?"

"Yeah, *Chicago Herald*. Why?"

"That's awesome news, bro." Shoving a microphone and earpiece into my hand, the cameraman stepped back a foot and said, "Just go ahead and give me a quick rundown of what's going on. In your own words."

"Are you fucking with me? I said I work for the *Chicago Herald*. You know, a newspaper? The thing you lined your pet rabbit's cage with as a kid? The stuff you tore up and used to make papier-mâché in art class? Jesus."

"I know, I get it man. But my reporter got carried away in the crowd. We go live in thirty seconds. Please, bro, I need your help or this is gonna look really bad."

"Go live? You mean you have a working satellite uplink?"

"Yeah, why?"

I was probably the only journalist in the country who hadn't figured a way around the government communications blockade.

"So you're gonna help me out, right?" the videographer asked anxiously.

"What? No. I've got to do my own job, I don't have time to do yours, too," I replied.

"Please, bro, I need this. This is my shot, and I'm going to get blamed for it if it fails."

Blinking away the tears in my eyes, I saw an unkempt young man wearing a filthy ball cap and look of desperation I recognized from my early days as a reporter. Newspapers were a tough business to break into and succeed at, but broadcast journalism was on a whole different tier reserved for those who embrace masochism and self-flagellation—the people who derive some sick joy from being crushed beneath a constant pressure to produce compelling content on unrealistic deadlines, and wish to do so while showcasing their failures in high definition to hundreds of thousands of viewers too stupid to read a newspaper.

"Fine kid. I'll give it a shot. But thirty seconds and I'm out. I don't care if you have to fake a bad connection, thirty seconds. Understood?"

"Awesome, man. You're the best," he said, adjusting his camera on his shoulder.

"You know you guys are on the verge of being replaced by bloggers with flip cameras, right?" I said, stuffing the earpiece into my ear.

"What?" He looked at me quizzically; then, touching his ear, said, "Shit, okay. Three, two, one..." he counted down with his free hand. My earpiece crackled as a male's voice rolled through the static.

"Now we go live to our reporter in the field, Wyatt Overstreet. Wyatt, how's it looking out there?"

"I'm afraid Mr. Overstreet had to step out for a moment—nervous bladder. This is Grant Cogar, your eye in the sky weather reporter with a special news bulletin: Here in Cairo, the natives seem to be gathering in the streets in some sort of strange tribal ritual. The youth of the city are gathering and throwing projectiles—found bottles and stones, mostly—at established authority figures in a peculiarly violent coming-of-age ceremony. Some are posturing—looking for a mate. Others, consumed by the vigor of the ritual, have begun to dance and cry out in strange tongues. Why, what's this? It appears they're gesturing for me to join them!" Dropping the microphone and flinging the earpiece at the horrified cameraman, I bounced away into the crowd.

Fucking broadcast news.

No doubt I just tripled their ratings. That clip would probably hit the Internet and end up on a late night talk show within the week. Kailas would be pissed. Not that I did it, but because I didn't introduce myself as a contributing writer for the *Chicago Herald* so he could filch some of the fame.

Circling back to the flagpole I'd been on the verge of climbing, I felt a tug on my belt. Looking over my shoulder, I found Perry ducking as a firecracker exploded just feet over our heads. I'd forgotten about him entirely.

"That was a dick thing you did back there," he yelled.

"What are you talking about? I did that kid a favor. Maybe now he'll pursue a more reputable and satisfying career in the janitorial services or prostitution."

As I turned back toward the tall steel beam swaying in the wind, Perry tapped me on the shoulder.

"Where are you going, Cogar?"

"Up. What does it look like?"

"Don't leave me here."

"I'll be right back," I said, securing my notepad in my pocket and rubbing my hands together. "You keep watch here. Take some notes. Throw a rock."

Like a chimpanzee, I planted my feet against the pole and began shimmying my way upward; keeping a wary eye on the army cordon as I climbed. The shouts of the crowd swelled in volume until they became an almost deafening roar. Reaching the flagpole's zenith, I looked around at the miles of people flooding into the streets and leaning out of windows in the buildings surrounding the square—the broiling waves of bodies punctuated by those holding the red, white, and black Egyptian flag over their heads. Fireworks thrown toward the cordon popped and screamed, bursting dully and contributing to the smoke already thick on the air. The two-note wail of ambulances and fire trucks echoed under the people's booming shouts.

From here, it seemed impossible to doubt that this uprising would eventually see success—the army cordon appeared to be little more than a dark island at constant risk of being flooded. Gripping the flagpole tight with one hand and squeezing hard with my crossed legs, I reached into my pocket and withdrew my phone. Bringing up the camera function, I snapped a few photos of the crowd and the barricade; then, holding it out and up, I aimed it at myself, grinned, and snapped another photo. That one would go into my personal collection.

Normally I'm more careful about how and where I take photos for stories. In countries under the control of a dictatorial regime—such as Egypt—you'd be surprised how many buildings turn out to be military or clandestine government installations. Officials get kinda ornery when people take pictures in the vicinity of those buildings, even if they really are just admiring the architecture. With the advancements made in commercially-available tech— smart phones, digital cameras, and GPS to name a few— it's easier than ever for a spy to blend in and look like just another tourist snapping a digital photo to send home to mom.

These governments find it best to act cautiously and assume everyone is working for their enemies.

At best, you may have your gear confiscated.

At worst, *you* may end up confiscated.

Man, am I hearing things, or is it getting even louder out here?

The cries and shouts of the protesters had grown to such a thunderous roar that the earth itself began to shake; the flagpole rocked gently to and fro, its halyard slapping against the metal loudly. And it suddenly occurred to me why: The protestors had seen me, and they thought I'd climbed the pole to tear the flag down in an act of defiance.

This was bad.

Another key principle I've learned as a battlefield reporter, and one of my personal guiding, cardinal rules: Report the news—don't become it. Maintaining neutrality and focusing on being an observer rather than a participant is not only a good way to go about reporting, but lends itself nicely to surviving, too.

The zigzag streams of the fire hoses shifted toward me, the water losing its velocity as it traveled through the air and landing harmlessly near my feet, dripping down. Recognizing the army's attempt to shake me from my perch, the crowd lunged forward with renewed fervor. The soldiers quickly turned their attention back to the masses threatening to burst through the barricade.

I should get down before I get shot down.

Tucking my phone into a shirt pocket and buttoning it, I attempted to gently slide my way back to earth. Suddenly, my feet slipped on the now-wet post, and I lost my grip. Amidst surprised shouts from those below, I tumbled head-over-heel, my stomach lurching as I plummeted helplessly toward the earth. I never cried out, nor did I see a parade of my multitudinous lovers dash across my vision. In fact, I think I only gritted my teeth and awaited the sudden darkness when my head would burst like a ripe melon against the asphalt below.

Suddenly, my leg—heretofore waltzing with the halyard on my way down—became entangled in the rope. I felt my skin shredded to a red pulp as the rope halted my travel abruptly—my head mere inches from the unforgiving earth.

"Jesus Christ, Cogar, are you okay?" Perry shouted, running toward me and untangling the rope.

"Wait!" I shouted a second too late. Falling abruptly the rest of the way to the concrete, I landed heavily on my shoulder and moaned.

"Whoops. Sorry, Cogar."

"Sure you are," I said, slowly returning to an upright position. The noise had become deafening, and as I shifted my gaze above the bobbing heads of the protestors, I spotted the reason why. Dozens of men mounted on camels rode into the crowd, clubs and swords in hand. These *baltagiya*—gangsters paid by the police to hand out rough justice without sullying the government's name—crashed into the crowd and slammed their weapons against the unprotected heads and shoulders of protestors underfoot.

"Cogar, let's get out of here before we get killed," Perry yelled.

"It's just getting good," I shouted in protest as a rubber bullet whistled past my ear.

"Please. For the love of God, use some common sense, Cogar. It doesn't do us any good to stay here. We've seen plenty."

"This is why all your girlfriends scream my name during sex," I chided as we dodged through the crowd, eventually making our way to an unoccupied alleyway a few blocks away. "There. Are you happy? For fuck's sake, Perry, I can't hold your hand through everything. Man-up."

"This isn't about manhood, Cogar. It's about knowing where the line is between bravery and stupidity. You were well on your way to crossing that threshold."

Taken aback by his comment, try as I would, I couldn't formulate a clever response.

"Nu-uh."

Rubbing my shoulder as we slowly walked away from the protests, I caught sight of two men on an adjoining street in my peripheral vision. They looked familiar.

"Oh, no way," I said, suddenly recognizing who they were. It was the Brotherhood's guards—the ones we thought we'd ditched at the hotel, and they didn't look pleased. I'd no more than pushed Perry's arm to alert him of the urgency in which we should flee when the big, bearded guard—still wearing his fuzzy red *tarbush*— noticed me staring at him. The giant pointed at us, and the two guards approached. I felt a nervous pinch in my stomach as I slipped off my suit jacket and reluctantly unbuttoned my shirtsleeves, rolling them to my elbows.

"Is this because I didn't bring you dinner like I promised?"

The men neared, hands balled into fists.

"Gentlemen, I was just on my way to the airport," Rothko said, trying to find a place to hide his equipment.

"Shut up, Perry, and grab something heavy."

Now for those who have never been in a street fight before, it's key to remember this: Fights don't go down like they did in your father's generation. You don't shake hands with your adversary the next day and you don't laugh off fresh lacerations over beers. The fact is, people are a whole lot angrier and more vindictive than in years past. Fights don't end when you touch the ground; in fact, you can pretty much count on your attacker putting his heels to you long after you've given up or been knocked unconscious. So, fuck Queensberry rules, fairness, and mercy—they'll only serve to get you beaten to death and left for the police to scrape off the pavement with a snow shovel. Losing a fight is no longer a matter of pride, but a matter of life and death. So feel free to fight dirty—your opponent will.

"You've got the big guy, right, Perry?" I said, pointing toward the larger, bearded aggressor.

"Like hell!" Perry responded as he backed toward a wall, fists held timidly before his face.

The smaller attacker sprinted at me, listing toward the building to my left as he ran. Leaping from the ground with a vertical that would have quickly put him on an NFL talent scout's radar, the man planted both hands against the wall, tucked his knees to his chest, and swung his hips until his legs were vertical, his head pointed at the ground. I watched in awe as he spun himself completely around, landed lightly on his feet, and, without missing a step, cast himself into the air again—rolling his feet over his head like an Olympic gymnast, his body spinning a full 360-degrees. Suddenly kicking outward, the heels of his shoes struck my chest squarely. I tumbled to the ground, my head striking the brick hard and the familiar taste of blood filling my mouth.

Fighting for breath as I attempted to regain my feet, I groaned, "Brotherhood…hiring…fuckin' monkeys now?"

"It's called Parkour," Perry yelled as he slipped away from his yeti-like opponent. "The art of displacement. Street gymnastics."

I didn't care what it was called. I only knew that the one big advantage I'd had in almost every fight since high school had been my agility and speed. This guy had me trumped on both counts. I spat as I fought my way to my feet, a string of blood-laced saliva painting the dust-covered bricks.

Monkey Man took a long step toward me, swung his arms behind him, and projected himself into the air once more—his legs swinging about his torso like a helicopter's rotors. Not wanting to stand around waiting to receive another impressively choreographed strike, I leapt toward my adversary, hands up and protecting my head, shoulder aimed for his chest. The collision brought both of us to the ground together.

Diving toward my adversary, I managed to plant an elbow against his bearded chin. Undeterred by the strike, the little bastard flipped me over his head and was on me so fast, it took me a second to realize I was in a chokehold—the man's knee firmly against my back. His sinewy arms pulled tight around my throat, and I wheezed as I struggled for breath. Blackness crowded the edge of my vision as I started to slip from consciousness. Reaching a hand over my head, I felt for the ridge where the man's upper lip met his nose and pinched with every ounce of strength I had left. It was an old trick I had learned in a bar fight in college—the nerve clusters beneath the nose are very near the surface, and when irritated, cause involuntary tears.

Crying out, my attacker reached a hand to remove mine from his face—the opportunity I needed to turn my hips, break his grasp, and slip a punch into his groin.

It's kinda my trademark move.

Pulling myself to my feet, dust from the scuffle hanging on the air, I looked over to check on Perry's progress. Lifted off his feet and held firmly by the knot of his silk tie, Rothko was repeatedly thrown against the side of a nearby building—all the while imploring his aggressor to have some decency.

In my peripheral vision, my antagonist slowly raised himself to his feet again, a quivering rage playing across his features as he gasped for breath. Still struggling to see through the tears in his eyes, the man leapt toward me with a new and equally impressive display of acrobatics, his right leg coming about mid-flight on perfect course with my head. Jumping as high as I could, I let the guard's kick find my ribs, but wrapped my left arm around his calf and held it tight to my side. Slamming the palm of my right hand against his jaw set his body into a flat spin, the man's arms coming up in search of something to pull him upright. We both hit the ground hard, but he took the worst of it—my body weight landing entirely on his leg. I heard a loud, fleshy *thump* as his back struck the bricks.

Pushing myself away from him, panting wildly and massaging my ribs where a fresh, foot-shaped bruise was forming, I watched in a sort of dismayed amazement as my attacker brought his knees to his chest and exploded outward, bringing himself upright again as though the six foot drop hadn't shaken him at all.

"I'll give you this much, you are one determined sonofabitch," I said, dropping my fists into a boxer's stance. I swung a hard left hook toward his kidneys.

Though he blocked my shot with his forearm, my right hand shot out and took firm hold of his beard. Pulling hard to the left, I guided his head into the first floor window of the adjacent building. The glass shattered, and my attacker slumped unconscious—his body arched atop the windowsill.

Shaking the dizziness away as I picked the fresh shards of glass from between my knuckles, I turned my attention to the big man attacking Perry—just in time for the ape's fist to catch me squarely on the jaw.

It felt like I'd been struck with a baseball bat. I found myself lying on the ground, looking up in confusion with the giant towering over me. I kicked my heel toward his knee, but he caught it and twisted it fiercely. An electrical pain shot up my thigh, hip, and back. Taking a step back, the man heaved me like a shot put—tossing me a full ten feet by my ankle. Landing heavily, the air rushed from my lungs in hopes of finding less violent habitation.

I was used up, I knew—in no way, shape, or form prepared to fight this brute. I heaved and tried to force breath back into my chest as I began crawling toward the busy street, hoping someone would help me.

I could hear the big man's booted steps as he followed.

Flipping to my back, I confronted the giant as he prepared to bludgeon me with a piece of rusty angle iron he must have found in the alley. Internally I was kicking myself for not discovering the instrument before he had. I might have had a chance, then. Any time you can swing the odds of winning a fight in your favor by using a found object—trashcan, brick, or tire iron—to disable an opponent, especially a bigger or more-skilled one, do it. Even if you're feeling confident you'll win, there's no point in needlessly breaking knuckles. Of course, adopting this mindset as I have means you can't be too upset when your opponent beats you to it.

Desperate, I aimed my pointer finger at him and raised my thumb, yelling, "Hold it. Not another step or I'll drop you where you stand."

The giant paused, momentarily confused by my childish reaction, then snickered—spitting a wad of rust-colored saliva at my feet, a rivulet running through his beard.

"I mean it, not another step."

The big man raised the steel above his head and I flinched away.

A gunshot rang out.

Looking first at my pointer finger, and then at my attacker, I noticed a three-inch hole in his right breast—his eyes glazing over as he collapsed to his knees, his lifeless upper body dropping heavily into my lap.

Shoving the corpse aside and pulling myself to my feet, I whispered, "Perry, did you see that?"

Looking around for my rival, I suddenly realized a small crowd had gathered. Most were tattoo-covered, some wearing prison uniforms. At their front stood Kek, the fringes of his black eye patch turned white from dried sweat. Moving the smoking pistol in his hand to the back of Perry's head—my rival struggling to stand upright, bobbing in place as he fought unconsciousness—Kek hissed, "Nice shot."

10

Get Some Sun

"You tampered with my food, didn't you?"

Perry's voice shook me from my thoughts. Tied back to back around a concrete pillar, my adversary and I were both clueless as to our location—our shirts had been torn from our chests and tied to cover our eyes by Kek and his men just before we were thrown into the bed of a pickup truck and hauled here. The smell of gasoline, the hum of fluorescent lights overhead, and the echoing effect of our voices suggested we were being held in a cavernous garage of some sort.

"Why do you say that?"

"You know why. That was childish."

"I'm not saying I know what you're talking about, but if I did, I would argue that it's better to have a juvenile sense of humor than to be a compulsive liar and a thief," I said.

"What's that supposed to mean?"

"I really shouldn't have to explain it to you, Perry." From the depths of the building, the eerie, scraping sound of a heavy steel door being shoved open reverberated off the concrete walls. "Sounds like our friend is back."

"How about you let me do the talking this time, Cogar? You always find a way to make them even more pissed off whenever you open your mouth."

"This coming from the guy who almost got both of us killed back in the Sudan because he couldn't keep his trap shut? No, I'll take my chances."

"Christ, Cogar. When are you going to let that go, huh? It was ten years ago. Grow up."

"It was seven years ago, Perry. And no, I won't let it go. You didn't think you burned a few bridges by stealing that article from me?"

"I didn't steal it from you."

"What would you call it? Borrowing without intent to return it? At best it was barefaced plagiarism."

"I didn't borrow it or plagiarize it, either. You and I were working together on the assignment. You did *some* of the research that helped me to write *my* article, and it turned out to be good enough for a Livingston Award. You're just mad that your work wasn't considered—and I get that—but you need to make your peace with it. That angst is going to eat you up inside."

I bit my lip and breathed out slowly. "I didn't know you won a Livingston Award."

Perry's voice softened. "Yeah, that's why the *Times* hired me."

"I see. Congratulations, that's quite the accomplishment."

"Thanks, Cogar. That means a lot coming from you."

"You fucking piece of lying horse shit, you don't deserve to be mentioned in the same breath as the Livingston Award. You ripped me off, you ignominious hack. And you dare to relegate me to your fucking research assistant? I completely wrote that article without an ounce of help from you. And what's worse, you were too lazy to even change the language—you literally took the paper out of my hands, my unconscious fucking hands, and walked it right into Kailas's office pretending like it was all your own doing. If there's any justice in this world, that crazy Syrian guy is going to sodomize you into a coma."

The door leading into the garage swung wide and smashed loudly against the wall as heavy, traipsing footsteps approached us. I felt my shirt ripped from my head. Kek, a battle-worn AKS-74 rifle slung over his back, stood before me, a large garbage bag—ready to rip from the weight of its contents—wrapped up in his left hand.

"Great, you're here. I need you to kill this guy for me," I said, nodding over my shoulder toward Perry. As my eyes adjusted to the dim fluorescent lighting, I finally took a hard look at our captor. "I never thought I'd say this to someone who lives in the Middle East, but you should think about getting a little sun."

Taking a moment to digest what I had said as he pulled Perry's head cover off, Kek suddenly snickered, replying in broken English, "No iron. Makes pale like you." *An iron deficiency.* Maybe his condition would make him weak enough for us to overpower him. That is, if he was dumb enough to give us a chance, which he had proven already, he was not.

"You know, Kek, you seem to have an unusual attachment to this idea of killing me. I mean, you murdered two of the Brotherhood's guards—guys on your side—just so you could be the one to end me. What gives?"

"Game never escapes hunter," he said nonchalantly, digging in the garbage bag. Tossing a rusty crowbar, duct tape, and a dirty IV line attached to a bag of saline or sodium chloride on the oil-stained concrete floor, Kek finally found what he was looking for—a battered, handheld video camera. He smiled devilishly as he propped it on the hood of a tire-less car mounted on concrete blocks a few feet away.

"See? See what I mean about making things worse every time you open your mouth?" Perry whimpered.

I couldn't see my rival, but I knew he was thinking the same thing I was. We had just been exposed to a well-known occupational hazard—a nightmarish scenario that every reporter, though never openly acknowledged, dreads: A sadistic lunatic with a political agenda had captured us, and he had just pulled out a video camera. I had seen plenty of videotaped pleas by fellow reporters who never made it back home—at least not in one piece. The recording invariably precedes the severing of one's head and first-class postage of the dismembered part to the unsuspecting family. We were in deep shit.

Kek stepped around us slowly. "Japan, World War Two, American GIs capture, like you now," he said in his rasping, almost unintelligible voice. "Japan soldier hungry, no food, so take knife," he said, withdrawing a laughably short blade from his pocket and removing its leather sheath. "Cut piece of GI to eat." He slid the knife's spine along my cheek, and with a flick of his wrist, slashed a shallow wound perfectly parallel with my jaw. I was startled by the speed at which he'd cut me and by the absence of pain—the blade I just dismissed must have been as sharp as a surgeon's scalpel.

He continued, "But, Japan soldier have no refrid, refrid…"

"Refrigeration?" Perry offered.

Kek wheeled around, smashing the back of his hand against Perry's temple, sending the reporter reeling—his body weight dragging me around the pillar and putting me face to face with our captor. Without the slightest sense of rage or anger, our captor resumed his story as though the interruption had never happened. "No refridaration. So Japan soldiers, they cut good; no kill. Keep GI alive long time to eat. I study—know to kill GI slow, like Japan soldiers."

"You can read?" I said.

Raising his hand to strike me, I shifted my weight hard to the right and spun around the column, dragging Perry in front of Kek's fist in time to receive that hit, too. Grabbing hold of the ropes that bound our wrists together, our captor yanked me back to face him. His one functioning eye, jaundiced and expressionless, stared through me.

"All joking aside, you are exceptionally pale," I said, moving my face as far from his as my restraints would allow.

Kek opened his mouth, revealing an irregular row of cracked yellow teeth, some filed to sharpened points.

"I take your man parts first."

If ever there was a more succinct expression designed to shut a guy up, I haven't heard it. I swallowed hard as I tried to think of a way out of losing my closest traveling companions.

"Need tools, first. Hold please," Kek said, raising his knife. With a deliberate thrust, he plunged the blade into my shoulder—the steel piercing through skin and muscle, the tip lodging in the bone. Before I could even cry out, he had turned and begun digging through his garbage bag for what I could only imagine were far more sinister tools. I don't know if my cries were from the pain flooding from my arm or the knowledge that far worse was soon to come.

"Fuck, Perry, he's gonna kill us. We are royally fucked," I moaned as blood trickled down my arm, flowing around the wooden knife handle.

"Hang on, Cogar. I've got a plan," he said reassuringly.

"This isn't the time for jokes," I cried, trying not to stare at the assortment of rusty, medieval-looking instruments Kek was casually sorting through.

Gathering his tools in one hand, Kek turned and approached me slowly. Suddenly, I felt Perry pull his body weight around the pillar, scooting me away from our captor as a high-pitched cry—like that of a martial arts instructor mid-strike—filled the air.

From the corner of my vision, just before the concrete support blocked my view, I saw Kek's elbow shoot up instinctively. And just like that, I found myself sliding back toward the mercenary, fresh blood from Perry's nose making a speckled trail around the pillar.

"Great plan, Perry. Thank God you were here to save me."

Perry coughed loudly and blew through his nose, a sickening, phlegm-like sneeze echoing through the room. "Better than just letting him kill us," he said between moans.

Kek reached for my shoulder and removed his knife, intentionally twisting as he withdrew it. Though I tried to stay silent—not wanting to give him the satisfaction of knowing the pain he was causing—the tearing of flesh forced an involuntary cry from deep inside

my chest. A quick left hook to my ribs stopped me mid-
scream as I doubled over, gasping for breath. Sliding his
knife under my belt, Kek set about unfastening my pants.

"Didn't you see my promise ring? You'll have to
wait until we're married," I wheezed, driving a knee into
the Syrian's chin. Skittering backward on his hands, Kek
hissed like an injured snake. Ignoring the array of
unusual, primitive-looking tools scattered about, he
grabbed the crowbar from the floor, leapt to his feet—
shockingly spry considering his sickly countenance—and
rushed toward me, sharpened end angled forward, ready
to impale. I froze; unable to decide which side I should
dodge to in order to avoid the unpleasant addition of an
extra orifice. My attacker was nearly upon me, and all I
could do was watch through wincing eyes, awaiting my
untimely demise.

Just before the tip of the pry bar reached my skin,
a figure stepped from Perry's side of the pillar and,
swinging what looked to be a car's axle shaft like a
baseball bat, struck Kek squarely in the forehead. The
Syrian's legs came up and the back of his head slammed
against the icy floor, his limbs sprawled wildly on the
ground.

The man turned toward me and set to work removing my restraints.

"Sabi? Holy shit, man, I got you all wrong. You're back on the Christmas list. Big kudos on the timing, too— if you had shown up a second later, that crazy bastard would have had me looking like a pig on a spit," I said.

"I'm not spiteful enough to leave someone, even my enemy, in the hands of that *ibn himar*—son of a donkey," he said, gesturing toward the unconscious Kek. "But you should really thank my sister—she convinced me to come after you. For reasons beyond my understanding, she seems to like you."

"Aqiylah's your sister?" I said incredulously as I reached to put my shirt back on, gingerly sliding it over the still-bleeding wound in my arm. I suddenly understood why he'd been so protective of her.

"What did you think she was? My girlfriend? Hurry up—let's get to the car. She's waiting for us, and I don't know how many guards Kek has around here. They're bound to come looking for him soon."

Perry interrupted, "First of all, who the hell are you? Are you with the revolutionaries?"

Sabi turned to me, perplexed.

"He means the Muslim Brotherhood," I mumbled, tearing a sleeve from my shirt and wrapping the fabric around my wound as tightly as I could stand.

"Who?" Rothko asked.

"This isn't the time, Perry. You can play 'Twenty-one Questions' when we clear out of here."

"Well shouldn't we, you know, make sure he doesn't follow us?" My rival reached to the floor and slowly pulled up a jagged piece of broken concrete.

"What, you're going to just bash the guy's brains in like some kind of bloodthirsty ape?" I asked.

"No, you are," he said, trying to hand me the stone as I pulled my hands away. "You're the one he's after."

"No way, dude. I'm not into cold-blooded killing. Doesn't agree with my fragile sensibilities. Might give me nightmares."

"If you don't do it, he'll come after us again. Only this time he won't be so protracted in his efforts to kill us." Perry stared at me with a look torn between concern and defiance.

I shook my head as I stared at Kek's unconscious form. "Not a chance."

"So, mister battlefield hero isn't so tough after all. I figured as much. Just like everything else in your life, Cogar, you're all talk."

He let the stone drop at my feet, turned, and walked toward the open door. Just like that, the suspiciously repentant Perry that had emerged since arriving in Cairo reappeared with all the familiar traits of the old, loathsome Perry.

"I'm all talk? How many scars from bullet wounds and shrapnel are you sporting these days, champ? I'm a goddamn charter member of the battlefield blood-donation club, you petulant fuck."

Standing beside me, Sabi said quietly, "Killing Kek would make you too much like him."

I nodded as I stared daggers at Perry, who had opened the door slightly and begun scanning the outside for Kek's men. "I didn't come here to make trouble, you know? I'm not out to murder anybody or to disrupt a political movement, I'm just trying to do my fucking job without getting killed." I was hungry, angry, and my arm hurt like a motherfucker. Perry was trying what little patience I had left.

"Maybe it's time you changed your technique," Sabi replied dispassionately. "Whatever you're doing now isn't working."

"You may be on to something there," I said, walking over to the car hood where Kek had set his video camera and slipping the device into my pocket.

"What do you want with that?" Sabi asked.

"Just a souvenir for later. I'd be interested to see what our friend here has been up to."

As we exited the building, Perry and I were forced to shield our eyes against the harsh sunlight. A white sedan with a checkerboard-like band on the doors and a yellow sign affixed to the roof sat idling nearby. A spiderweb crack covered most of the rear window, held together, it seemed, by faded bumper stickers and decals. Even at a quick glance, the vehicle's tires appeared completely tread-less, worn so smooth that one good divot or pothole would have certainly flattened them all.

"That's your escape vehicle?" Perry asked, blinking as he tried to look at Sabi. "A taxi?" I could understand his distrust: Experience has taught me to always select a taxi by the age of the cabby and the condition of his vehicle. In countries such as Egypt, where rules of the road resemble something out of Mad Max and emphasize natural selection via vehicular suicide, cabbies, like soldiers, only live to be old by being good at what they do. Sabi was young and the condition of his car seemed to reaffirm my beliefs on the subject.

"What's wrong with it? I can drive that better than you could any other vehicle."

"You haven't had the meter running this whole time, have you?" I joked as I tenderly touched the wound in my arm. He could have showed up on a pink tricycle for all I cared, so long as it got me out of here.

"For you, you bet your ass it's running. As far as I'm concerned, it's been running since I dropped you off at your hotel this morning. Do you have any idea how hard it is to get gasoline here?" Eying my wound, he continued, "And so help me, if you leave blood on my seats, I'll kill you."

11

Tough Enough for a Battle Beard

"So how'd you find us?" I asked as we followed Aqiylah and Sabi up a narrow flight of stairs leading to their apartment. Perry walked close behind, his head held high in the air as he sniffed back his still-bloody nose. Located in the plainly downtrodden *Manshiyat Naser* district a few miles east of the Nile and my hotel, this building, nearly hidden among the countless drifts of swollen garbage bags, was little more than a crumbling two-story structure faced by a few dusty, cracked windows and topped by overlapping sheets of rusty tin. It smelled strongly of a floral perfume and appeared clean despite its decaying outer shell. Notwithstanding, I could tell Aqiylah was embarrassed to have us here—it wasn't a flattering reflection of her country or her circumstances.

"I was with Kek when he got a phone call from the guards telling him of your escape. He didn't seem angry, but excited."

"After seeing him put a bullet through his teammate just so he could be the one to kill me, I know exactly what you mean," I said.

Sabi reached into his pocket and pulled out a key ring as he continued. "When the guards found you, they contacted him again. I followed him, let him capture you, and waited until I was certain he was alone with you at the garage before attempting a rescue."

"Well, again, I appreciate you doing that," I said quietly. "He would have killed us for sure; he even gave us a detailed outline of how he'd go about it. The guy's kinda creative in a sadistic, sociopathic sort of way."

"And again, I'm telling you, if it weren't for Aqiylah, I wouldn't have done it. We may very well have spoiled our relationship with the Brotherhood by coming to your rescue," Sabi scolded.

"Hardly," Aqiylah scoffed. "Don't listen to him, Grant. Kek is a lunatic. If the Brotherhood knew that he'd disobeyed his orders with plans to kill you, they'd have wanted us to stop him. Have you seen the way El-Shafik looks at him, Sabi? He knows just as well as we do that Kek is unstable—if not handled carefully, he's likely to turn on him, too."

"Yes, well Kek isn't dead—and he's as sure to come after us as he is to hunt you down, now," Sabi said, stopping in the stairway and casting me a sullen look. "Fucking American journalists."

182

I smiled at him insincerely and changed the subject. "Maybe you guys can shed some light on this for me," I said, raising my fingers to the bridge of my nose and squeezing until the pressure overcame that of my growing headache. My arm pulsed with a steady, exhausting pain; the knife wound would turn septic if I didn't address it soon. "You think you need the Muslim Brotherhood's blessing to overcome Mubarak, right? I mean, that's how we were introduced—you captured me because you thought that would put you in their good graces. But it seems to me that when Perry and I were in Tahrir Square, nobody was singing the praises of the Muslim Brotherhood or wearing their membership badges proudly on a sleeve."

"Nobody is going to openly declare their allegiance to an illegal organization," Sabi replied coldly, resuming his journey up the stairs. Our footsteps clamored dully, reverberating in the narrow space.

"That's fair. But this whole thing got started with inspiration from the uprisings in Tunisia, right?"

"You could say that the Tunisian protests were the catalyst, I suppose. Mostly, they were a sign to our people that such an uprising could ultimately succeed," Aqiylah said from behind me.

"Right. And the Tunisian uprising was almost entirely youth-driven. It was successful because it was organized, and it was organized because nobody knows how to use social media and the Internet like today's youth."

Irritated, Sabi turned to face me again, standing before the door to their apartment. "What's your point, Cogar?"

Fed up with Sabi's indignant responses, I turned around to look at Aqiylah. She glanced up at me and smiled knowingly. "My point is you guys don't need the Muslim Brotherhood to succeed in bringing about a democracy here. You two, and others like you, *are* the uprising, not the Brotherhood. When all this settles, I think history will relegate them to little more than a footnote."

Aqiylah and I stood quietly looking at one another; only the sound of Sabi working the door's turn bolt interrupted the silence.

Reading my facial expressions and looking over Aqiylah's shoulder, Perry suddenly realized that she was a woman, and a particularly beautiful one at that. He sniffed back as much blood as he could and butted between us to introduce himself.

"Aqiylah, is it? I don't believe we've had the pleasure of an introduction. My name's Perry Rothko—I'm a reporter with the *New York Times*." He emphasized that last part: a simultaneous effort to impress Aqiylah and insult me. I don't know about the former, but it certainly worked to piss me off.

Perry flashed his trademark high beam smile as he reached to shake her hand. I figure he must be one of the only people in the world who could walk into a dentist's office, have them take one look and, returning their tools to the tray, say with surprise, "Damn. Looks good. See you in six months." To my surprise, Aqiylah shook his hand softly. She looked at me out of the corner of her eye before responding, "It's a pleasure to meet you, Mr. Rothko."

"Please, call me Perry."

Stepping through the door to their apartment, Sabi immediately sat down on a worn loveseat, kicked his feet atop an overturned milk crate, grabbed a remote and a pack of cigarettes, and turned on the television. Flipping through the channels as he tapped a smoke out and lit it, he stopped upon arriving at Al-Jazeera's news coverage of the uprising. Though the picture was spotty and the anchor spoke in hurried Arabic, I could tell that things had only continued to escalate since we'd left Tahrir Square.

"Perry, can I speak with you in private for a moment?"

"No, you can't, Cogar. God knows what'll happen if I'm left alone with you again—I'll probably end up getting abducted or beaten," he laughed snidely, looking back at Aqiylah as she pulled the door closed behind us.

Pushing him into the apartment's small galley kitchen, I whispered, "Let's get this straight right now, Perry: You stay away from that girl. The last thing she or any of us needs to hear is you and your corny-ass come-ons."

"Whoa, whoa, whoa there, sport. What, you think you're the only one who recognizes a beautiful woman when you see one? What gives you any right to speak on her behalf?"

After a split-second consideration, I decided that the reason I wanted Perry to keep away from Aqiylah was primarily because I didn't want her to get hurt by his philandering, but also because I wanted the bastard to be miserable and lonely whenever possible.

"Because I know why you're coming on to her, Perry. You saw that she has a thing for me, and, like a child, you can't stand to see me with something you don't have."

"So you two are in a relationship of some sort?"

Flustered, I stuttered, "Not exactly, no."

"Then I don't think your argument holds any water, Cogar. She's not a thing, anyway. You can't *own* her. Why don't you man-up—as you said to me a few hours ago—and play the game?"

"I'm not competing with you because it's not a fucking game, Perry. Just stay away from her, okay? Simple request."

"Then I'll respond with a simple answer, Cogar. No."

Aqiylah, stepping around me in the narrow entryway, gently touched my shoulder with her hand—just letting me know she was passing. I winced as the crippling pain shot up my spine. Turning back and looking at me with concern, she asked, "How badly are you hurt?"

Tenderly sliding the blood-soaked fabric away from the wound and pulling down on my shirt collar, I exposed the deep knife wound in my shoulder.

"Grant," she cooed softly. "Go into the bathroom and sit down. I'm going to get the first aid kit and patch you up."

I turned and gave Perry my best 'fuck you' grin before turning and following Aqiylah.

"So you're a doctor now, too?"

"I've had to put in my fair share of stitches before. You're not afraid, are you?" she taunted.

"Lady, I've had more stitches installed in me than you've had years on this earth. I could probably put them in myself."

Actually, though I've indeed received plenty of stitch-worthy wounds in my life, I still hate needles, and the notion of sewing flesh still gives me the heebie-jeebies. I'd met Special Forces guys in Afghanistan—the battle-beard-wearing, thousand-yard-stare types—who unflinchingly stitched up their own wounds as though they were mending a tear in their uniform. Needless to say, I'm not like those guys. I could only picture myself crying like a little girl as I hesitatingly poked myself with a threaded needle.

I stepped into the bathroom with Aqiylah, and she gently closed the door behind me.

"Sit here," she said, gesturing toward the toilet as she moistened a hand towel. "Take off your shirt."

I followed her instruction. "Sounds like I owe you an enormous debt of thanks for persuading your brother to come save us."

"He would have saved you anyway; don't let him convince you otherwise."

"I'm not so sure, Aqiylah. He doesn't seem to like me very much." I lowered my voice. "In fact, he's kinda behaved like a malicious prick since I met him." *Considering our first meeting concluded with him drugging me, I'd say that's a fair assessment.*

"You don't know him the way I do. He's a good man and a hard worker. He spends mornings working at the coffee shop; then drives taxi until late in the evening. He pays for this place and most of our mother's care. As if that weren't enough, he spends what little free time he has actively working toward political change—bringing about a democracy for Egypt. I admire him a great deal, and you should, too."

"It's hard to admire a guy who's working so hard to get me to leave his country."

"He just doesn't trust you yet. Not like I do," she said quietly, dabbing the towel at the coagulated blood fringing the wound in my arm. Her words triggered a glow in my chest for some inexplicable reason. But I reminded myself that, though it was well and good that she trusted me, I still shouldn't fully trust her in return. Sure, she'd saved me from Kek. But if she hadn't drugged me at the coffee shop, I wouldn't have even been on the sick bastard's radar. Moreover, I'm a firm believer in the 'fool me once, shame on you—twice, shame on me' ideology. She may have deceived me before, but I'd be damned if I got caught off guard twice. Aqiylah had already made clear that she valued her cause more than our friendship. No doubt that hadn't changed, and the last thing I needed was to be bartered away as soon as it became advantageous for her to do so.

After a moment of closely inspecting the bloodied tear in my arm, she said, "This is really deep, Grant. We should probably take you to a hospital. When was the last time you had a tetanus shot?"

"A couple months ago, I think. I get a medley of vaccinations and antibiotics each year. You just never know what new avian flu is getting passed around in remote corners of the world, or who's going to stab you and whether they bothered to clean their knife beforehand."

"Do you want me to stitch you up here?"

"Go for it. Let's see what you've got," I said confidently while my self-conscious screamed, *Are you out of your fucking mind? Don't let her do it!*

"This is going to hurt, you know. I don't have any anesthetic."

"Yeah, I know," I said in my gruffest baritone.

Leaving the bathroom momentarily, she returned with a threaded sewing needle bent into the shape of a J. As she carefully punctured one edge of the wound, a sharp, burning pain crept up my neck. I bit my lip and squeezed my hand into a tight fist as she slid the steel through to the other side and pulled it taut, blood pooling around her fingers.

"Why don't you give me something to keep my mind off your knitting? Tell me about the neighborhood—seems like an interesting place," I said between clenched teeth as I struggled to take a full breath.

"Okay." She paused and sighed. "Well, there was a rockslide a few years ago that killed a hundred people just a little up the road from here."

"Jesus you people are grim."

"You wanted to know about the neighborhood. I'm telling you about it," she said, continuing her explanation as she expertly slipped the needle beneath my skin again. "The government knew it was a dangerous area long beforehand, but chose to do nothing. That's their way. And when the inevitable happened, they dismissed it entirely. Today, the survivors still live and sleep in that same high-risk area atop the buried bodies of their lost family, stowed away beneath high voltage power lines and awaiting another rockslide."

"Why do they stay?" I asked, sensing the pain in her voice.

"Because they have no other choice. They have no money to go anywhere else. The average wage in Cairo is 360 pounds a week. Sixty American dollars. Now consider that this neighborhood is far poorer than most of Cairo. They call it 'garbage city' because the only jobs to be had here include sorting through trash for things to recycle. There's no public infrastructure: When people need a toilet, they dig a hole; when they need water, they get it from contaminated wells, usually feet away from the latrine their neighbor just used. If there's electricity, it's been stolen. A million people packed into an area of less than five square miles, Grant. It's squalor."

She snugged the next stitch especially tight and I gasped, my eyes burning with tears.

"Maybe this was a bad idea, Aqiylah. Why don't you just hum a tune or tell me about the local sports scene, instead? Or camels. Tell me about camels. Do they actually spit, or is that a myth?"

"I'm sorry, Grant," she said, wiping her bloodied hands on a rag. "It's just hard to sit by and watch these people—good people—narrowly survive when I know that others in the government are enjoying tremendous extravagance, and don't care if those beneath them live or die."

"I get it, really. But you're kinda hurting me."

"Why don't you grab my leg and squeeze if the pain gets to be too much?" she asked innocently.

We looked into each other's eyes as she slowly moved my hand up her leg. I felt a smile work its way to my lips, a nervous tingle humming beneath my beltline as I gently moved my fingers against the fabric covering her inner thigh. She continued to sew the wound closed, the pain fading to a tolerable throb as I sat and admired the way her tongue would peek out from between her lips when she became really focused. Tying off the last stitch, she said, "There: all done. You did great." Patting my cheek, she whispered, "You make a good patient."

"I've had plenty of practice," I said, reluctantly sliding my hand from her thigh to her knee before moving it back to my lap. "You did great, too, Doc. That'll make a wicked-cool scar."

She looked at me with a confused smile. "You're weird."

"Yeah, people keep telling me that."

"But I like you."

"I like you, too."

From the living room, Sabi shouted, "I'm going to work. I'll be back in a few hours." Sticking his head into the bathroom, he looked at Aqiylah and said, "Stay here." Turning to me, he whispered, "And you and your friend? You even think about touching her, and you'll wish I'd let Kek have his way with you. Understand?"

Glad that I'd removed my hand from her leg a few seconds before, I raised my arms in the air. "You don't have to worry about me. That one, though…" I said, gesturing toward Perry. "Better to keep an eye on him."

Sabi grabbed his keys and donned a light jacket before jogging down the stairs. I knew where he was going, and it wasn't to pick up fares for his taxi service. He was running back to the Brotherhood to tell them what had happened and to turn Perry and me in. He may not have wanted to see us killed, but he didn't want us running free, either.

"We should go out," I said to Aqiylah as we joined Perry in the living room. "Grab something to eat." I was also in no mood to wait around to be recaptured.

"And then let's go dancing. Sabi never lets me dance," Aqiylah said, tugging on my arm.

"Lets you dance? You're a free woman; you should be able to dance with whomever you want, whenever you want," Perry said, buffing out a fresh scuff in the toe of his Berluti loafer with his thumb. For once, I couldn't have put it better myself.

Aqiylah blushed and smiled at him. "It's not like it is in America. Things are a little different here." She shrugged and sighed. "Well we don't have a car, so we'll need to walk. But I know a great spot not far from here where we can grab a bite to eat and meet up with a few friends. She reached into a pocket and withdrew her phone, sliding it open and rapidly punching keys. I looked at the device suspiciously. It seemed odd that Aqiylah would in one breath decry the destitute conditions surrounding us and in the next, call her friends on such a luxury as a smartphone. I decided the good folks at Muslim Brotherhood's regional office must have given it to her as a free, no-obligation sign-up gift to facilitate communication.

"I'll let them know we're coming. You'll like them."

"No doubt," I said withdrawing my phone from my shirt pocket and checking for reception. "You have cell service, too?"

"Of course. Why?"

"Orabi said they'd shut down the Internet and cell towers last night. I couldn't get any kind of reception from my hotel this morning, and I can't now."

She raised an eyebrow and smiled dubiously.

"Seems odd. I must just be lucky."

She'd been perfectly aware of the government's efforts and had found a way—like thousands of others, undoubtedly—to bypass the state-controlled networks.

"Lucky. Right."

As I waited for her to finish her message, my eyes wandered to the black cigarette stains coating the ceiling above the loveseat. Suddenly remembering Kek's video camera in my pocket, I reached for it and tossed the device onto the sofa. It would end up lost or destroyed if I kept it with me. Looking down at my dirty, socked feet, I asked, "Does your brother have a pair of shoes I could borrow, by chance?"

12

Karma's Shot to the Groin

"Aren't you two cold?" Aqiylah asked, wrapping her arms around her middle and burrowing further into her jacket as we walked along broken pavement leading into the city proper.

"Back in Illinois, a winter's night is about 50 degrees colder than this. I'm sure it's the same in New York, right Perry?"

He ignored me as he slid his suit jacket off and wrapped it around Aqiylah's shoulders. "How's that?" he asked.

"You didn't need to do that, Perry," she said. "But thank you for being so considerate."

Dammit. Why didn't I think to do that?

Simple. You left your jacket lying in a carefully folded pile in the alleyway where you boxed it out with the Brotherhood's guards. No, don't worry about it now; it's gone for sure.

As much as I didn't want to look at Aqiylah as a prize in Perry's little contest, I was losing to the slick bastard. And if she were a prize, she was the finest a man could hope to compete for. She'd left her *hijab* behind at the apartment, and in the minutes before we left, applied makeup beneath her eyes, let her hair down, and dabbed on perfume that smelled subtly of citrus and jasmine. I watched, enthralled, the confident sway of her hips as she walked.

"I'm in the mood for Shawarma. You?" Perry asked.

Surprised by his sudden cultural awareness, Aqiylah replied, "Sure! I know just the place."

Adjusting his gait to match mine and leaning toward me, Perry whispered, "Women like a man who's not afraid to take charge. Pay attention and you may learn something today."

"You patronizing prick. Keep it up and you're going to learn how my shoe tastes," I whispered in reply.

He laughed and patted my shoulder as though we'd only been bantering amiably. That made it worse—making me wonder if I was just being too thin-skinned.

We arrived in short order at a street awash in the glow of streetlights and neon signs, a bustling district filled with thriving restaurants and shops, the black night sky interrupted by large backlit billboards.

Spotting her friends nearby—a small group of mostly teenage men and women—Aqiylah exchanged embraces before introducing Perry and me, naming our publications and the states from which we came. When her friends heard the words "New York", they became instantly taken with Perry. As they filled the night air with overlapping questions in Arabic, Aqiylah began rapidly translating.

"They want to know if you've been to Broadway, and if you ride the subway everywhere."

Perry smiled and stepped forward, fully embracing his sudden celebrity-like status. Narcissist.

"I do ride the subway, and the *New York Times* building is only a few blocks away from Times Square and Central Park. I go running there over lunch most days."

He runs to stay in shape. I run to stay alive.

The small crowd watched his mouth move, entranced. Aqiylah waited for Perry to finish talking before translating to her native tongue. I watched her intently as she spoke and listened to the musical range of her voice. But I wasn't staring so attentively as to miss Perry casually slipping a hand against the small of her back, his pinky finger resting at the top of her shapely behind—showcased in a pair of flattering blue jeans. I felt a wave of jealousy as I realized I'd been entirely forgotten. I was of no real interest to anyone here. And it suddenly dawned on me that for all these years, I'd been wrong about Perry: He *was* a better reporter and *was* more interesting than me—not because either of those things was really true, but because he was so damn good at pretending they were. Perception is everything.

Stepping away from the crowd quietly, I set out down an adjacent road, kicking at rocks and admiring the night sky as I contemplated what my next step should be. I needed to put Perry and Aqiylah out of my mind, I knew. Despite being an attractive and good-natured woman, Aqiylah was ultimately a distraction that was keeping me from getting my story finished. Perry—as he has always been—was little more than a shit stain on the underpants of life, and I needed to stop letting him get to me.

I was here to do a job, after all. I'd gotten a few good quotations so far, and an exceptional photo from the flagpole incident that would work for my article. So why was I still here? I should have been back at my hotel, typing like a madman to get the article done and shipped back to the States. And when it was complete, I would move on to the next assignment, and Aqiylah and Egypt would fade to a distant memory recollected only by a digital photo of me on a flagpole and the scar on my arm. Which reminded me, I still had a homicidal maniac on my tail. The last thing I needed was to get too comfortable going about my business and forget about Kek. He had already proven that he wouldn't be deterred from his quest to kill me, and Sabi's interruption was most certainly not the end of the Syrian's manic pursuit.

A soft yellow glow from a basement-level store, smoke rolling out the one open window near the street, caught my attention. Following a short stairway down, I opened the door to a small *shisha* lounge. This wasn't the cleanly kind built for tourists, with video game consoles and a dinner menu at each table. This one was dark. Musky. The curtains, carpet, and seats all wore the same smoke-dulled, threadbare crimson fabric, illuminated by antique light fixtures and strands of red Christmas lights. Half a dozen middle-aged men, all bearded and many of them missing teeth, looked up at me curiously. Looking around uncomfortably as I massaged the wound in my shoulder, I turned to leave. Before I could, one of the patrons, his dark skin so deeply wrinkled it resembled dried mud, stood from his cushion and approached me slowly, extending his hand. He guided me toward his cushion and gestured for me to sit. I tried not to look distrustful. But I was. Though the air smelled heavily of vanilla-scented tobacco, the men here were up to something else—their eyes, even through the haze of the smoke and the dim light, were bloodshot and glossy, pupils constricted to black pinpricks.

The man to my right, his legs crossed and one hand twirling his chest-length beard, slid the *hookah's* mouthpiece—attached by hose to a swirled glass base in the group's center—from between his lips, holding it out to me and grinning.

"No, thank you. I'm more of a cigar man," I replied, holding my hand up. The man nodded, slipped the mouthpiece between his teeth, and, with the bubbler still puttering softly, swept aside the folds of his robe and withdrew a plastic strip of pills. Motioning for me to hold out my hand, he thumbed one of the pills into my palm.

Taking a strange pill from a strange man in a strange country isn't wise practice, obviously. *But not taking it might be worse*, I thought as I noticed the man by the door fondling a Browning Hi Power pistol and staring at me skeptically.

When in Rome.

Palming the drug onto my tongue, I swallowed forcefully and smiled, as did my new friends—revealing their eighteen collective teeth. Within minutes, a warm, comforting feeling emanated from my core. Opiates. I'd been given opiates. At first, the sensation was a welcome one, the pain from my many wounds fading to a subtle throb. But that soothing feeling quickly gave way to one of anxious unease. I needed to get out of here. Depending upon the strength of the drug I'd been given—which I doubted even my dealer knew—I could continue to just feel warm and fuzzy for a couple hours or I could pass out in the next sixty seconds, before I could get back to Aqiylah or the relative safety of the street. I'd heard some crazy stories about opportunistic men in sexually repressed societies, and I didn't want to test their validity here.

"Grant?" I sat straight up. Aqiylah approached cautiously through the smoke, trying to make out my form in the shadows. "I wondered where you went."

Combing my hair with my fingers nervously, I smiled and said, "I thought I'd take a stroll. Meet some new people; these guys seemed awfully friendly." I tried not to reveal how stoned I was. My lips felt dry, and I found myself clumsily enunciating each word. "Where's Perry?"

"I left him with my friends. They're good people—he'll be okay. A few of them speak enough English to keep him entertained for a while." Aqiylah spoke quickly, made uncomfortable by the seedy nature of the place and its strange, unsightly inhabitants.

"They won't need to speak; he won't let them get a word in edgewise."

"He *is* talkative. But then again, you aren't so quiet yourself," she said as she sat down beside me on a cushion, folding her legs and leaning against me. She still wore Perry's jacket. I wanted to tell her all the reasons why she should avoid falling for my adversary, but reminded myself again that it wasn't my concern. "You two aren't so different, really," she added, watching the men pass the pipe around the circle.

"That's an awful thing to say."

"Why? You two have a lot in common. Even your mannerisms aren't so different. Both of you are full of such bravado, but beneath that, you're caring and gentle."

I laughed sarcastically. "I'm sorry, but you're wrong. He's just putting on a show to impress you. You don't know what he's really like."

"But I'm sure you do," she said, turning to me with a frown.

I wasn't helping my case. She'd taken a shine to Perry, and despite the fact that she'd woefully misjudged his character, my telling her so was only going to make her think I was jealous or mean-spirited. That didn't stop me from continuing.

"Yeah, actually, I do. He's been a pain in my ass for close to a decade. The only thing that's changed in that time is he's gotten better at hiding his manipulative side," I said, moving my feet until the tingling in my legs disappeared.

Clearly insulted by my differing judgment of Perry, Aqiylah changed the topic, "You know, you should be careful. Wandering the streets alone as a foreigner right now may not be safe."

"What are you talking about? This is the most fun I've had since getting here. Hanging out here with these old fellas, we're safe as houses."

"I'd like to leave now," Aqiylah said waveringly as she met the eyes of the man across from her. He hadn't averted his stare since she'd entered.

"I was just on my way out when you came in," I said, tugging her to her feet.

The others stood with us.

"Thanks for a fun time, fellas. Poker at my place next week?"

One of them grunted, rubbing his thumb and pointer finger together in the universal sign for money owed.

"Right, payment." Sliding my billfold out, I tossed the last few bills I had onto my cushion, bowed toward my new friends, and began steering Aqiylah toward the exit, still warily following the hand of the gunman near the door.

The man who'd invited me in reached out and grabbed my wrist with a surprisingly strong grip. He shook his head as he pointed to the cash on the cushion. Revealing the black abyss between his teeth as he smiled, he gestured toward Aqiylah.

Payment.

This meant trouble. Aqiylah gripped my arm with renewed zeal.

"Seems like a fair trade," I replied cheerfully, retrieving my money from the seat.

"Fair trade? Grant, what the hell are you doing?"

"Just trust me, okay?" I said under my breath as I pried her fingers loose.

"No! Do you have any idea what they'll do to me?"

I ignored her and headed towards the door alone. The men laughed sadistically, their voices raspy and heavy with smoke.

I didn't want to fight again—the knife wound in my arm still ached despite the drugs, and the bruises from my fight with the Brotherhood's guards felt pretty damn fresh. But it looked as though that was the only way we were getting out of here.

Stopping at the door beside the armed guard, I withdrew a few Egyptian pounds and tossed them into his lap. "Just a little something for your troubles," I said. He looked at me and grinned, a cigarette poking out from between his lips.

I slammed my open palm against the burning tip of the cigarette, driving it into the back of his mouth. Before he had time to react, I brought my forehead against the bridge of his nose, a subtle cracking-egg-sound emanating from the point of contact. As he choked on the smoldering cigarette, hands held to his face as blood flowed between his fingers, I grabbed the back of his head and drove my knee into his chin.

"Who's next?"

I had held no illusions that our antagonists weren't going to let us leave peacefully—it was better if I got in a few good shots early in hopes that doing so would reduce their numbers and give Aqiylah the chance to flee.

Reaching for the fallen guard's pistol, I thumbed the hammer back, sighted it on the chest of the biggest man in the room, and pulled the trigger. Expecting plenty of noise and muzzle flash, imagine my surprise when the hammer clicked loudly as it fell into place. Looking from the weapon to the robed man now gripping Aqiylah by the throat, I asked, "Doesn't anyone in this country own a decent gun?"

The men rushed forward like Viking berserkers, screaming as their arms flailed wildly. Gripping the Hi-Power by the slide, I whipped the pistol into the chest of the nearest man. He groaned and gripped his sternum as it connected, collapsing to the floor with a gasp. Three others continued the attack, closing the distance and grabbing me before I could throw a punch. The last went for Aqiylah—tackling her into the cushions and upsetting the *hookah* as he tore at her clothes. She cried out and brought her hands against his neck as he groped her.

Even martial arts experts will tell you that fighting multiple enemies at once presents several unique challenges; not the least of which stems from the fact that even two weak enemies still equate to more than one powerful one: You're now faced with dodging four fists coming from two directions rather than two coming from one. And for each additional opponent you add to the mix, the collective strength of your attackers rises exponentially, and by result, your likelihood of winning, or surviving, drops precipitously. Add to this the fact that my attackers were higher than a giraffe's ass and couldn't feel pain if their legs were dangling inside a wood chipper, and suddenly my odds of winning seemed especially slim.

With two men holding my arms, the third began working my ribs like a punching bag. Kicking out, I managed to push the junkie-turned-Floyd-Mayweather to the floor. Twisting my upper body, I planted my left heel into the groin of the man to my right. With my right arm suddenly free, I centered my fist on the face of the attacker to my left. Wasting no time, I leapt atop the man assaulting Aqiylah. Wrestling him away from her, I rolled him onto his back and buried my elbow in his larynx.

"Aqiylah, run!" I yelled, grabbing the *hookah* and shattering it over the head of an approaching attacker before being pulled back, the remaining three men grabbing my shoulders and resuming their assault.

Left hook to the ribs.

Right cross to the jaw.

Left uppercut to the kidneys.

I groaned as knuckles slammed against my skin, my legs sliding out from under me. But the men holding my arms kept me upright despite my best attempts to collapse. I couldn't breathe. My teeth split the skin inside my mouth and warm blood flooded under my tongue.

Though I didn't see it, I felt the man on my left briefly lose his hold as Aqiylah leapt atop his back in an attempt to free me. The world was growing dark, and even if I'd had the strength left to fight, it was unlikely we would be able to overcome their numbers. I wished Aqiylah would listen to me and make a run for it, but I couldn't muster the air to make my appeal again.

Before I passed out, I heard one of the men cry out, "*hattasil bel-bulīs!*" My body dropped to the floor as the room emptied.

When I awoke a few minutes later, two Egyptian policemen knelt over me; Aqiylah's head rested on my chest as she listened for a heartbeat.

"Those candy-asses run off? Just when things were getting lively," I mumbled, a warm stream of blood trickling down my cheek.

Aqiylah looked up and laughed, but her eyes were filled with tears. She hugged me gently.

One of the policemen reached to his shoulder and pressed the push-to-talk button on his radio transceiver. I held a hand up to him.

"Not necessary. I'm okay. I appreciate you guys coming to help, but if you think I look tough, you should see the other guys."

"Sir, you should get medical attention," he said in broken English. They both appeared nervous, which at first made perfect sense—two policemen out on a night like this would make prime targets for the many disgruntled bands of protestors. I felt worse for them than I did for myself. That is until later, when I realized the only reason they would have barged into an opium den is if they were already planning on being there—probably to score something for themselves or collect on a protection fee.

"Naw, I swore I'd never touch the stuff. You wouldn't happen to have a smoke, though, would you? It's been one of those days."

Bewildered, the policeman looked to his partner, shrugged, and reached into a pocket to withdraw a pack of Cleopatra cigarettes. He carefully placed one in my mouth and lit it. I smiled and shook both the men's hands. It'd been a close call.

"You guys can get on with your night. I just need a minute to lay here; you know, build up my strength." I could feel the start of swelling in my cheek from one of the blows, and my chest felt as though I'd been tenderized with a rubber mallet. I was going to hurt for a month after this trip, I knew. But calmly puffing the cigarette, I ran a hand through Aqiylah's hair. I'd received worse beatings, and those hadn't ended with a beautiful woman holding me close.

13

Fine Red Mist

Aqiylah walked me back toward Perry and her friends, my arm draped over her shoulder. It had taken some effort to get me upright. I felt 40 years older and a few pints low. Nothing a soft bed and three or so days of uninterrupted rest couldn't fix, but it wasn't likely that I'd be getting that any time soon.

"You should have run, you know," I said.

"I wasn't going to leave you there. You know me better than that, Grant."

"I guess I do now." I felt remorseful for doubting her. Anyone willing to stick around and fight by my side against overwhelming odds deserved my trust.

"That was stupid to fight them. You're only one man," she said, resting a supportive hand against my chest. "I'm starting to think you're a little reckless."

"I'm not reckless, I just get backed into corners a lot. Besides, what other option was there?" *You make it sound as though this was an unpredictable accident—you wandered into that opium den on your own, you know.* I cleared my throat uncomfortably and continued, "There's no telling what they would have done to us if I'd given them time to think about it. I figured forcing their hand would throw them off a little and give you a chance to escape. I just didn't want to see anything happen to you. Speaking of which, are you okay?"

"I'm fine." She looked up at me, smiled, and rested her head against my shoulder. After a few moments where the only sound filling the evening air came from our shoes crunching atop broken glass and pebbles, she said, "Thanks for looking out for me, Grant."

"Ditto."

Perry and his gang of captivated listeners hadn't moved far from their place. My rival sat on the roof of a pickup truck, the others kneeling in the bed looking up at him. His voice low and dramatic, he recounted in extensive detail how he'd narrowly avoided death at the hands of rebel Tutsi militants during the Kivu conflict in the Congo. The story was one of his favorites to tell at cocktail parties and media events and grew more implausible each time he told it.

"And as I stood before the mighty Bagaza, sweat dripping down his thick brow—surrounded by a dozen armed, swarthy men eyeing me like a piece of fresh meat—I stepped forward, grabbed his gun, and moved the barrel over my heart. I said, 'If I'm going to be killed today, you'd better be the one to do it.' The old boy smiled at me, handed me the rifle, and said—"

Stopping mid-sentence upon seeing us, Perry exclaimed, "Aqiylah, are you okay?" He leapt from the truck, pushed my arm off her shoulder, and, holding both her hands tenderly, looked her over for damage.

"I'm fine," she said, gently pushing him away. "Grant's been hurt, though."

"I'm okay too," I lied. "Just another day as a tri-country bare-knuckle boxing champion. Everybody wants to unseat the champ." I gingerly shadowboxed an invisible opponent. "Next week, I take on Pakistan's best: Farag the Dog. Heard he was born without fingers—he just has clubs made of scar tissue and barbed wire."

"You've really gotta kick that drug habit of yours, Cogar."

"Perry, if I was using, do you think I would've ever left the poppy fields in Afghanistan?"

Explaining the fight we'd been in to her friends and excusing us, Aqiylah led us back toward her apartment. I hesitated.

"You know, Aqiylah, I think I'd rather just go back to my hotel. We can catch up some other time."

"Cogar, did you hit your head or something? That's exactly where the Muslim Brotherhood will be looking for us. And correct me if I'm wrong, but wasn't that Kek guy part of that organization? You think he's done looking for you?"

I shook my head, frustrated. First, yes, I did hit my head—repeatedly against a guy's fist. Second, I didn't want to return to the apartment because I knew Sabi would be waiting for us there with more of the Brotherhood's foot soldiers. At best it would mean deportation, at worst, extended imprisonment. I'd had enough of both attempts to last me a good long while. But I knew if I were to voice my concerns to Aqiylah, she'd take it as a personal slight. She trusted that her brother had our best interests in mind, and though I could appreciate that display of trust, that didn't make her less wrong.

"The Brotherhood knows where you and Sabi live, right?" I asked Aqiylah.

"Not exactly. They know the neighborhood, but none of them have been to our home before."

She wasn't grasping my concern. Every part of me was screaming to leave right then and there and strike out on my own. Perry, thinking he'd finally get his chance alone with Aqiylah, would wind up captured by the Brotherhood and booted out of the country. Meanwhile, I would be free to pursue my story. Hell, I could even send a query to the *Times*. Boy, that'd stick in his craw, seeing my byline on an article he was supposed to have written for *his* newspaper. But, as appealing as that prospect was, I couldn't bear the thought of seeing the betrayal on Aqiylah's face, particularly in light of what we'd just been through together. So I continued to trudge forward, taking in the smell of her hair as she helped me along and kicking myself for being so foolish.

"I'll tell you what, Grant. Let's wait for Sabi to get done tonight, and we'll take you back to your hotel. It'll save you on fare, and maybe you can show me around when we get there?" she asked timidly. "I've never been inside the Conrad. I've heard it's nice."

"It'd be my pleasure," I answered dully, fully aware of how unlikely me getting back to my hotel that night was. "The place has a great view. Beats the hell out of sleeping in a fighting hole."

"What's a fighting hole?"

"A defensive fighting position. The Marines call them fighting holes, the army calls them foxholes."

"Did you serve in the military?"

"No, I just tagged along and wrote about the guys who did. I spent a year in Iraq when I was fresh out of college and another three in Afghanistan. Even met Prince Harry when I was in the Helmand Province."

"*The* Prince Harry? Of Wales?"

"Tall, ginger royalty, more hair than his brother? Yeah. That's the guy. Had a cup of coffee with him in the mess tent. You know, he's actually a pretty stand-up fella; not afraid to get his hands dirty on the front lines, but soft-spoken and modest, you know? Just one of the guys. You'd like him."

Perry sneered, disbelieving. I couldn't hold that against him—Harry was the stuff of legend. A boy born into a life of castles, steeds, and stuffy British royalty, attends the Royal Military Academy and requests deployment to the front lines in Iraq. When refused on the basis being a high-value target, the young prince says he would sooner leave the army than see his regiment deploy without him. I'm sure he said it in a delightfully candid, heavily accented English fashion, too.

In response to this refusal and as a show of solidarity, British troops began wearing shirts emblazoned with the words 'I'm Harry'—much the way Kirk Douglas's men stood up and announced 'I'm Spartacus!' in the film of the same name—as if to confuse the enemy and make their comrade less of a target in a tongue-in-cheek sort of way. It seemed to work. A year later, somebody spilled the beans that Harry had spent the past few months in Afghanistan fighting it out with the Taliban alongside the rest of the ground pounders.

I had to trade a dozen MRE fudge brownies, a gently used Penthouse magazine, and half a bottle of Templeton Rye to a lance corporal for one of those shirts, and I'm convinced someday it'll be worth something.

"That's so awesome, Grant. I'm only two degrees of separation from having met a Prince!" Aqiylah said excitedly.

God, she was young. I could just envision her squealing loudly upon seeing the British heir to the throne, begging him to sign his name on her chest.

Suddenly remembering her other companion, Aqiylah turned to Perry and asked, "Have you been on the battlefield, too?"

"I've spent my fair share of time in a flak jacket," he said stoically, as though sequestering nightmarish recollections of bloody battles and lost comrades he'd buried himself. It was probably best that the few working streetlights were widely interspersed, and no one could see me roll my eyes in disbelief. Perry had about as much battlefield experience as anyone who had seen live footage taken from soldiers' helmet cams on YouTube. If he had ever been near a battlefield, he'd never left the relative safety of a forward operating base, and had only heard shots fired in anger as distant echoes.

I don't doubt it sounded impressive to Aqiylah—it painted a vivid picture of an armored soldier bedecked in MOLLE gear fearlessly staring down enemy fire, not that of an overdressed journalist wearing a bright blue life vest with the bold sans serif letters PRESS lining its front. But most of the grizzled veteran journalists I've met, with the exception of a stubborn few—cowardly egotists with an inflated sense of their self worth, usually—insisted on *not* wearing a ballistic vest.

Perry wore his to bed.

"I've never been a fan of flak jackets," I said, running my tongue along my teeth, checking for new gaps and missing pieces.

"Oh come on, Cogar. Now you're just arguing for the sake of arguing. There's nothing subjective about wearing protective gear."

"Sure there is. For instance, you like them because they may, and I do mean *may*, stop a bullet from giving you a new orifice. That's cool, but they almost always fit like an off-the-rack tuxedo and weigh a ton."

"It's negligible weight."

"Not negligible when it comes to adding seconds of exposure to enemy fire. If you and I were to race, and you had a vest on but I didn't, I think I'd have you beat by more than a few steps—even with all that yoga and those runs through Central Park under your belt. Those few steps could mean the difference between flying home economy class or in a box."

Perry looked at me with a tired expression, raised his eyebrows and looked away. I got the message—he wasn't looking to argue. It'd been a long day for both of us. But bickering with Perry felt oddly therapeutic. It distracted me from the smoldering doubt, the little warning voice sounding all the alarm bells in the back of my mind telling me to run back to my hotel, or to that youth hostel I was going to stay at originally. Hell, at this point, even going back to that little opium den of a *hookah* bar would have been a smarter move than heading back into the trash-lined streets of *Manshiyat Naser*. "Besides, ballistic vests are indiscreet and unnatural-looking, so they make you stick out in a crowd and remind every unprotected indigenous civilian of your life's superior importance to their own."

Yes, my survival is essential enough to warrant body armor. No, yours is not.

Now run along and play "find the landmine" with your friends.

"Then why do soldiers wear them if they're such a detriment?" Perry countered.

"Because they're in uniform and are already perpetual targets. A journalist, if they know how to dress discreetly…" I looked at Perry disapprovingly as he adjusted the gold watchband at his wrist, "…and keep their mouth shut, can stay off the radar of most jihadists and enemy snipers. As far as I'm concerned, a ballistic vest is counter-camouflage."

Perry shook his head. "I don't agree. The downsides just don't outweigh the benefits in my eyes. If I have the option of putting a few layers of Kevlar between me and a piece of shrapnel for a couple thousand dollars and the risk of not blending in, I'll gladly take it."

I shrugged. He made a reasonable argument. But there was another reason I didn't care for ballistic vests that went beyond practicality. One that had put a bad taste in my mouth I just couldn't shake. I thought better of sharing it. It wasn't a story I recollected fondly.

Back in Afghanistan, during a mortar strike against our outpost just outside Kandahar, I watched a foreign correspondent—a German guy in his mid-20s—die *because* he had a vest on. A Taliban technical—a glorified pickup truck with an old Russian DShK heavy machine gun mounted to its bed—rolled by our outpost at six in the morning, dumping lead indiscriminately into the camp. Bedecked in a new, sparkling-clean flak jacket—the German guy, who'd been smoking a breakfast cigarette outside the fence when the explosions started, was slow to get into cover behind the HESCO barrier. A 12.7x108mm slug caught him in the chest, piercing his unprotected armpit. Trapped inside the jacket, the bullet bounced from one ceramic plate to the next, perforating his insides and turning him into a human sieve. You ever played racquetball? Imagine that rubber ball is a hunk of lead the size of a spark plug, and the enclosed court is a man's thoracic cavity. Yeah, it ain't pretty. It took him about twelve seconds to bleed out. Without the vest, he may still have died, but he would have had only one bullet hole to contend with instead of half a dozen. Admittedly, it was an unlucky and unlikely occurrence, but I'd still prefer to take my chances without a vest.

Approaching the familiar, crumbling outline of the Ibrahim's apartment building, I spotted a trio of shadowed figures in the street. The glowing cherry-red tips of their cigarettes hovered in the darkness like fireflies.

"Looks like your brother got home from work a little early," I said. I can't say I was surprised.

"Aqiylah," the figure in the middle shouted, "good work bringing them back. You had me worried; you're late."

Turning to her, I examined her expression, searching for any sense of surprise or sadness. Her face was vacant.

That…I hadn't expected.

She'd played me. Again.

I couldn't even be angry. I'd suspected what was going to happen, but chose to ignore my intuition. This was a painful reminder that I'd earned that gut feeling— those early warning signals that one only develops after narrowly surviving situations exactly like this one.

The familiar outlines of Kalashnikov rifles caught my eye in the low light, and my stomach tightened.

"You can go upstairs," Sabi said, flicking his cigarette butt into the dirt.

"Who are these guys?" Perry asked Aqiylah as she turned to leave. "Aqiylah? Who are they?"

"Who do you think they are?" I asked sharply. "Sabi went and asked his friends at the Brotherhood to come get us. She led us back here like fucking sheep. God dammit, I knew it. Why do you think I didn't want to come back here?"

"Well why didn't you say anything?" he asked, frustration and anger rivaling my own building in his voice.

"I figured my repeatedly pleading with you would have resonated. I should have known better to think you'd pick up on anything so subtle, you cretinous tit."

"Shut up, both of you, and get in the car," Sabi growled.

Aqiylah stopped walking, turned slowly, and returned to my side. She cupped my chin with the palm of her hand and kissed my cheek softly.

"I'm sorry this keeps happening. I know you'll never trust me again after this, and it breaks my heart. But you have to understand that I can't let my feelings for you get in the way of our mission."

"You're making a mistake," I said to Sabi, ignoring Aqiylah.

"No way am I getting in that car with you," Perry echoed my thoughts.

"That makes two of us, Sabi. You can take those rifles and shove 'em up your—"

"Enough! You're coming with us, or we'll cut you down here and now," Sabi interrupted, waving his two accomplices forward. "I want you out of my way for good."

"Yeah, okay. So you're going to shoot us after you risked your life rescuing us? I think you're full of shit," I challenged. "And you know what? You'll *have* to shoot me before you'll get me back inside that rolling piece of garbage you call a taxi."

The sudden deafening chatter from a rifle silenced our shouts and froze us in place as it broke the night air.

Wait, I didn't mean it. By all means, shoot Perry, but not me.

This wasn't part of the plan. Aqiylah wouldn't let them shoot us, would she?

But we weren't the ones catching the hot lead. Sabi and his two men twisted and convulsed in a macabre dance, slugs tearing through flesh and bone, casting a fine red mist into the night air. Seventy yards away, rifle tight to his shoulder and resting against the side mirror of a black Land Rover—the hood sun-bleached and the fenders pocked with rust—stood my old friend Kek.

Before I could contemplate why I was doing it, I dashed forward under fire, my pained limp disappearing as adrenaline flooded through my veins like nitrous oxide in a racecar. I slipped an arm under Sabi's armpit and heaved him toward safety.

"Leave me…leave me…" he sputtered, his eyes glazed over as blood dripped from a ragged hole in his ribcage.

"Don't give me any more reason than I already have to do just that," I said as the forceful wisp of a bullet blew by my ear.

By informing the Brotherhood of our whereabouts, Sabi had inadvertently invited my old buddy Kek to the party, too. He'd been ready to sell me up the river, and my vindictive side wanted to disregard the fact that he'd previously saved my life, drop him in the dirt, and run for it. But some part of me couldn't do it. Perhaps it was Sabi's words from when he'd saved us from Kek before: *I'm not spiteful enough to leave someone, even my enemy, in the hands of that son of a donkey.*

"Where's the car?" I shouted into his ear as the bullets from my antagonist's weapon rammed into the sandy earth at our feet, flinging dust and debris into the night air.

"Around...the...corner," he wheezed. Fishing the keys from Sabi's bloodied grasp, I tossed them to Aqiylah and said, "You drive."

Abandoning his attempt to shoot us as we passed out of sight, Kek began shouting orders in Arabic to what I assumed were his merry band of felons. I briefly wondered why Kek had been the only one shooting— surely the others would have guns, too, and if they'd all opened fire on us at once, it would have been a veritable firing squad. We all would have been killed.

Game never escapes hunter.

Suddenly, it dawned on me: Kek really was viewing this as some kind of twisted game where I had transformed from a human being to his prey. I was the fox, and he was the hound. He couldn't explain why he wanted to catch and kill me because it went deeper than logic. It was in his blood, pulsing through marrow and bone, organs and nerves. He needed to be the one who got the exclusive pleasure of killing me, because that was his self-appointed purpose in life.

Sliding Sabi into the front passenger seat of the car, I hopped in beside Perry in the back seat and screamed, "Let's get the fuck out of here!"

"I'm trying," Aqiylah said. The starter rattled with each turn of the key, but the engine indignantly refused to engage.

"Try harder," I shouted, squirming in my seat. "Goddamn piece-of-shit used-car-lot cut-rate-special taxicab."

Kek rounded the corner—his men following close behind. We had only seconds to get the car started before we'd be perforated with bullet holes and left for carrion.

Perry began to pray.

I began reciting every curse I'd ever devoted to memory. The list is not a short one.

Memories of vehicles I'd seen riddled with machine-gun fire during my travels—the bloodless corpses of the passengers, skin chalky and bloating as the car became an oven in the sun—came rocketing back. That wasn't the way I wanted to go. Not helplessly. Not like this.

14

Shoot the Bastard

Kek raised his rifle to finish us at the same time the dusty taxi rattled to life. The Syrian managed to fire a single round—the slug punching through the front windshield and centering the seat cushion between Perry and me—before Aqiylah slammed the shifter into drive, rammed the gas pedal, and ran directly through him and his men. Kek managed to tumble clear of the front bumper, but two of his crew slammed against the hood and were tossed over the windshield. Aqiylah spun the car wildly into the street, the smell of shredded rubber and exhaust flooding through the vents. Perry began hyperventilating as he pulled his knees to his chest and scrambled to get his seatbelt on.

"Dammit, Cogar...I should never have listened to you...I could have stayed in my hotel and...been on my way back to New York by now!"

"I don't want to hear it, Perry," I said, working quickly to tear open Sabi's shirt where the bullet had entered. His blood, warm and flowing rapidly, made it difficult to secure a good grip.

"Try not to bleed on the upholstery," I said sarcastically.

Sabi wheezed loudly—not entertained—blood bubbling from the wound with each breath. During my time on the battlefield, I'd seen similar wounds. Kek's bullet had ruptured one of Sabi's lungs, and the combination of blood loss and oxygen deprivation was especially deadly. "He's going to need a hospital ASAP," I said, pushing down on the wound with both hands.

"Oh, you fucking think?" Perry yelled, closing his eyelids tighter. "We're all going to need one if they catch up."

I turned to Aqiylah, looking more child-like by the second as terror overcame her features. Her hands gripped the wheel with white-knuckled ferocity as she navigated around slower-moving vehicles.

"Take a deep breath," I said, touching her shoulder with the less bloody of my two hands. Though I had every intention of harboring a colorful array of resentful feelings against her for her repeated betrayal, now wasn't the time for focusing on our personal quarrel. Not with Kek aiming to kill us all. "We'll get through this. Just get us to a hospital." Throwing a knee into Perry's ribs, I yelled, "You—shut the fuck up before I throw you out of the car." Slapping Sabi's cheek until his eyes opened slightly, I said, "And you'd better not pass out on me."

The sound of a big block engine winding up behind us caught my attention, and I craned my neck to look back. Kek's black SUV closed the distance between us. The butt of a rifle shattered the vehicle's passenger window from within, and through the opening, the Syrian emerged.

"Aqiylah? We've got new problems. You'd better step on it," I said, looking over my shoulder as the one-eyed brute pointed his weapon at our car. In my peripheral vision I caught a burst of muzzle flash as glass shards from our rear window rained down my collar.

Winston Churchill once said that nothing in life is so exhilarating as to be shot at without result. Exhilarating is the wrong word, and Churchill was a fucking lunatic for thinking that. The sensation is closer to 95 percent unadulterated terror and five percent relief that you've been granted time enough to take one more shallow breath.

Aqiylah, doing her best to keep the car on the road, reached into the glove compartment and withdrew the same Helwan pistol she'd captured me with before, slapping it against my hand. "Shoot him."

Tossing the weapon into Perry's lap, I yelled, "You heard her—shoot the bastard."

"Me? You've got to be out of your mind, Cogar. I can't shoot. I'm not a fucking soldier. You saw me at Colonel Orabi's house. I don't even like guns."

"Perry, if you don't put some fire on that Land Rover right now, I'm going to bludgeon you to death with that thing."

Reluctantly, Perry wrapped a hand around the pistol, thumbed its hammer back, and cautiously pointed it out the window. Behind us, Kek let the spent magazine drop from his AKS-74—a shower of sparks thrown by the aluminum box as it bounced along the pavement.

"Do it!" I urged. "You don't even have to hit him, just aim for the front of the car."

Yanking his index finger against the trigger, the pistol recoiled—a deafening crack filling the interior of the car, a sunburst of light exploding from the weapon's muzzle—then went off again instantly, the recoil of the first shot and Perry's inexperience causing him to fire again, the second shot heading toward the heavens.

"Jesus Christ, you're fucking hopeless. Give me the gun," I yelled, fighting the screeching ring in my ears as I yanked the weapon away and forcefully placed his hands against Sabi's wound.

"I told you, Cogar. I told you," he mouthed, his free hand held tight to his ear as he grimaced.

"How is it you've gone all these years in warzones without ever learning to shoot?" Preparing to lean out the window, I drew back inside as another long burst of 5.45x39mm rounds ripped into our vehicle, hitting in a ragged vertical line from the bumper to the roof.

It's worth noting that, unlike what you've seen in films where the bad guy's bullets spark and bounce off a vehicle's exterior, in reality even the smallest calibers can and will punch right through the car body's thin aluminum skin, plowing their way from one end of the vehicle to the other without much to slow them down.

Except for the people inside.

Consider that the next time you see a misinformed gangbanger driving with his seat pushed all the way back, peeking out from behind the door. It's good for a laugh.

Aqiylah screamed, and for a moment, I thought she'd been hit.

"Are you okay?" I asked.

"Make him stop shooting at us," she cried, terrified tears slipping down her face. Perry shared a similar expression.

"But have you been hit?"

"I don't think so."

"Scared the shit out of me," I mumbled as I leaned back out the window and clasped the pistol tightly with both hands—my right thumb resting atop my left, arms bent slightly, just the way I'd been shown by a couple of Army Rangers back in Afghanistan. Focusing on the front sight, I steadied the Helwan against our vehicle's frame and lined it up with Kek's pale, shining head, illuminated in bursts by the streetlights above.

You've never killed before.

Take him out. He's a murderer, not a freedom fighter or a soldier doing his job. He's just a killer, a rabid dog.

But you're not.

Do the world a favor and pull the trigger. Blow that bastard back to Hell where he belongs.

You've seen the fallout from the first kill—there's no going back. This will change you.

If you don't end him, he'll end you. Shoot now or you won't live to regret it.

I took up the trigger's slack; my eyes focused so intently on the weapon's front sight that Kek's body faded to a blur.

But just as the pistol leapt in my hands, Aqiylah cut the wheel hard to the left, jamming her foot against the brake to avoid hitting a line of protestors as they crossed into the streets. I felt the car lift from the ground, the world passing by in a haze as we were thrown against the vehicle's roof and tossed like ragdolls about the interior.

15

Life Debt

I blinked away the darkness. Covered in broken glass and shattered plastic car parts, I forced myself to move. Rolling slowly to a side and reaching a hand to support myself, I immediately let my body drop to the pavement again, crying out as crushing pain shot up my left arm. A cursory self-exam—conducted in the pulsing glow of the overturned taxi's hazard lights—revealed no protruding bone, but Aqiylah's stitching had come loose and gravel and road filth had embedded itself deeply into my skin. Satisfied that I'd survive my wounds, I let my head touch the road again. The muted sounds of stopped traffic and onlookers grew in intensity as I dozily took in my surroundings.

Our pursuers had stopped behind us, but were being held up by the crowd of protestors. Hands pulled me to my feet and gently dusted the broken glass from my back. Aqiylah and Perry were already on their feet, pulling the unconscious Sabi from the passenger's seat. Though bloodied and bruised, they looked to be in one piece.

Now where's that crazy Syrian bastard?

A shot rang out, screams filling the air as the protestors in the street flooded away from the sound. Amidst the running bodies, I spotted him; Kek stood with the butt of his rifle pinned in the crook of his arm, pointing at the sky as a wisp of smoke flowed from the muzzle. He waited patiently, surrounded by his men—his one-eyed stare unwavering as the people cleared a path between us. I wasn't going to wait for him to get a clear shot.

"Aqiylah, Perry, inside!" I yelled, gesturing toward a fortress-like building nearby. Running toward them, I slipped between Aqiylah and her unconscious brother, pulling his arm tight to my right shoulder. Sabi's body weight pushed down on my wounded arm, the pain forcing me to bite my lip. Perry and I lifted him up the stairs and through an arched doorway framed by two monolithic stone columns.

We crossed the threshold into the building just as Kek opened fire—his rifle chattering as missiles punched against the outside wall. We quickly took cover behind a display of terra cotta figurines and alabaster vases.

"Where are we?" Sabi wheezed, briefly returning to consciousness.

"Some kind of museum, I think," I said absently, watching the sweeping arch of the doorway for Kek's compact figure, wondering where the pistol I'd been holding had disappeared to. Looking down, I realized, dejectedly, that I'd lost my footwear again—the loose-fitting shoes I'd borrowed from Sabi had been tossed from the car during the wreck.

"Cogar, at the risk of you getting mad again and making threats against my life, don't you think that we're trapping ourselves in this place? I mean, if the army and police are too busy dealing with the protestors, who's going to come help us?"

Perry made a good point. One I hadn't considered during my panic-stricken efforts to escape the hail of gunfire Kek was pouring on. No doubt the Syrian mercenary had considered it, though. Even though the man was blatantly insane, he was also cold and calculating in his process. He'd use every second we had to wait for help to his advantage.

Aqiylah held a hand to her temple, her head bobbing. I looked at her, concerned in spite of myself, and gently touched her hair with my fingertips.

"You okay?"

"The crash rattled me a little, but I'm fine. Grant, what are we going to do?"

"We keep running until we've got nowhere left to run. If we can find a phone or a means of communication and a weapon or two, we can try to hold them off until help gets here. Aqiylah—your phone. Where is it?"

Reaching into her pocket, she withdrew the shattered remains of the device. Looking at me fearfully, she shook her head.

"That's looking like a tall order, Cogar," Perry said.

Kek's and his men's booted feet struck loudly on the limestone tiles as they entered the museum, the sound echoing as it struck the tall ceiling.

"Agreed. But now would be a good time to start that process," I whispered, ushering the others farther into the building's depths. "Stay low and stick to these statues," I said, gesturing toward the parallel rows of inert Egyptian royalty, religious figures, and gods carved in limestone. Pointing out an area that had been cordoned off for construction, I said, "There. We'll stop there—it looks like solid cover." Before we'd taken more than a few steps, Sabi, weaving in and out of consciousness, collapsed headfirst, Aqiylah crying out softly as she tried to control his fall to the floor.

"*Homa henak!*" Kek shouted to his henchmen as he opened fire with his weapon—the piercing cry of the security alarms masked by the crumbling of glass displays and the report of his rifle. Diving atop Aqiylah, I watched as fresh bullet holes appeared in the plaster wall above us. Beneath my chest, I felt her hand search for mine. Wrapping her fingers tightly around my wrist and moving her mouth to my ear, she demanded over the reports, "Kiss me."

"What?"

Before I could understand what she had asked, she turned to her side, wrapping her hands about my neck and sliding her leg against my groin. Pulling me against her, she kissed me hard. Her lips were dry and her cheeks wet from tears, but I didn't care. It was the most desperately impassioned kiss I'd ever felt. Instantly, all the resentment I'd saved up from her repeated betrayals disappeared, and I could only think about holding her lips to mine a second longer. Pulling my head to her chest, she yelled in my ear, "I didn't want to die without doing that."

The shots became intermittent as Kek's men fired to cover his reload.

"You're not going to die," I said, scanning the assortment of tools and construction equipment scattered about the floor. I would need one hell of an extension cord to make a circular saw into an effective weapon, I thought, kicking the tool away. Shifting my gaze to a nearby exhibit, I was suddenly struck with a plan.

Ducking low, I exited the construction area and approached a display showcasing the mummified remains of an ancient government official. The glass case surrounding the corpse had caught one of Kek's poorly aimed bullets and shattered. Reaching inside, I carefully unwound a foot-long length of the brittle linen wrap from the leg. *Sorry*—looking at the display, I read the mummy's name and information—*Senenmut. Tutor to Princess Neferure and confidant to the pharaoh Hatshepsut.* "Well, today hasn't been a total loss, I've learned something new," I joked to myself as I grabbed a dusty, wide-necked clay jar from the floor. A note card beside it indicated it held some of the world's oldest Teniotic wine. I sloshed the jar side to side, and convinced that it would work for my purposes, retreated back to Aqiylah and company. Bullets continued to perforate displays and drill ragged holes in the walls nearby. I watched from behind cover as Kek—thirty feet away and taking slow steps toward us—finished another magazine. With extreme dexterity and mechanical precision, the mercenary ejected the mag from his rifle, spun it 180 degrees, and slipped in the fresh magazine duct taped to the empty.

"Grant, they're going to kill us. We need to do something!"

"I'm all over it," I said, grabbing a screwdriver from a nearby toolbox and prying the hardened mud cap from the jar. The sudden outpouring of fermented stench caused each of us to gag.

"That's the most horrible…why did you bring that here?" Perry asked, pinching his nose tightly. I passed the jar beneath Sabi's nose, amused as he started awake, instinctively batting at the foul smell.

"Unconventional warfare, Perry."

Unscrewing the cap from an aluminum canister of mineral spirits left among a nearby pile of painting supplies, I emptied it into the jar and shoved one end of the mummy's linen wrap into the container's neck. Reaching for a propane torch inside a plumber's toolbox, I ignited the flame and touched it to the tip of the cloth.

"Un-fucking-believable, Cogar. You're making a Molotov cocktail out of priceless antiquities?"

"Open to better ideas," I muttered as I held the pot and the burning rag in an outstretched hand.

"There's no way that's going to work."

Standing up and dodging behind a pillar, I peeked out and spotted one of Kek's men—an emaciated, bald, heavily tattooed thug—standing in the open with an old bolt-action rifle gripped in his hands. I aimed for his feet, not looking to immolate the guy, just daunt him. The jar sailed over a row of artifacts and landed squarely on his toes, exploding into a golden chalice of flame. The man's screams rose above the cry of the security alarms as he dropped to the floor and rolled about in apparent agony. I winced. That had been a little more of a deterrent than I'd planned.

Slinking back to Aqiylah's side, I said, "That should send a clear message that we're not completely defenseless." A fragment of plaster, torn from the wall by one of Kek's rounds, stung my neck.

"But we are, aren't we?" Aqiylah asked.

"We are what?"

"Completely defenseless."

Pausing, I nodded. "Yeah, we are. But they don't need to know that. We just need to slow them down long enough for help to show up."

"You are unquestionably the single most insane person I've ever met," Perry shouted, Sabi's head resting on his shoulder as he clutched his knees to his chest. "And that's saying something considering we just got done being tortured by that murderous sociopath." He gestured toward Kek, who, fully aware he had us trapped, leisurely slid a new magazine into his weapon.

Leaning over Aqiylah, I punched Perry in the arm and asked, "Have you learned anything since our last fight?"

Rubbing his shoulder, he said, "Yeah, that I hate this country, and I'm not cut out for violence."

"Fine, help Aqiylah carry Sabi out of here. There must be a rear entrance. I'm going to try to slow them down."

"With what?" Perry asked.

Leaping toward a nearby wall—Kek firing a neat burst into the plaster near my ear—I plucked a spear from a decorative display and dove back into cover. Smiling, I said, "It only needs to be sharp enough to poke his good eye out, right?"

Another ratcheting cluster of rounds punched through a row of ancient manuscripts nearby—the neat calligraphy reduced to confetti, strands floating softly to the floor. Moving behind a stone column, Perry lifted Sabi's limp form and motioned for Aqiylah to join him.

"I'll see you soon, don't worry. These guys are really awful shots," I said. Sliding against me and cradling my cheeks in her hands, she kissed me again before moving to Perry's side. She looked back doubtfully as she reached for her brother.

Gripping the spear tightly with my uninjured arm, I stayed low and shifted around to our attackers' flank. Moving under cover of the alarms' piercing cries, I quickly approached one of Kek's thugs—his back turned to me— still proudly wearing his prison uniform. I eyed the SIG P226 he held near his hip and decided that I was ready to trade up from my primordial weapon to one with a little more snap. Changing my grip on the spear to one better suited to a baseball bat, I swung with full force, the stout wood handle finding the back of the criminal's skull and splintering on impact. A fresh pain shot through my injured limb—tears forming in my eyes as I cradled it gently and cursed. Breathing deeply and reminding myself that bullet wounds hurt more than a broken arm, I grabbed the fallen man's pistol and checked the action for a live round. I'd made the mistake of rushing into a gunfight with an unloaded gun before. Recently, in fact.

Looking up, I spotted Kek slinking among the exhibits like a lion amidst savannah grass. Dashing towards him, I managed to get within range just as he raised his rifle. He'd caught Aqiylah and her brother in the open. Perry was nowhere to be seen.

That cowardly piece of shit; he sacrificed Aqiylah and Sabi so he could make his escape.

I raised the pistol and prayed that whichever saint of marksmanship had guided my rounds back at the colonel's home hadn't stepped out for a smoke. Crying out, Aqiylah wrapped her arms around her sibling, protecting the wounded man with her body. Kek stood completely still. His hesitation seemed unnatural for a man so…unnatural. As I squeezed my weapon's trigger back, I suddenly felt something cold brush my head.

Something cold and cylindrical.

A rifle barrel.

Fuck me. I let my newly acquired handgun drop and raised my hands in surrender. One of Kek's men—likely the same one I'd lit on fire with my homemade incendiary grenade judging by the suddenly noticeable stench of burned flesh and fabric—had beaten me at my own game. I held my breath as I waited for the lights to go out and for my brain matter to be spread atop the museum's antiquities like manure over a bean field.

A dull clunk sounded, and the rifle barrel slid from the back of my head as a body collapsed to the tile. Turning around, I found myself face to face with Perry—my rival holding a stone tablet above the henchman's unconscious body. He wore a surprised expression that mirrored my own.

"Thanks, Perry," I stammered. I almost wished he'd just let the bastard shoot me. Now I owed Rothko my life. I can think of no worse burden for a man to carry than be indebted to his mortal enemy.

Before he could respond, a bullet tore a dime-sized piece of fabric from my collar. Instinctively, I dropped to the floor, pulling Perry down with me. I slithered along the smooth floor in search of cover, but faced with no quick escape, turned to meet my end.

Kek stood fifty feet away, his rifle trained on me. I looked from him to Aqiylah and back before making peace with my demise for the fifth time that day.

"Drop the weapon and place your hands on your head," a familiar voice barked from behind us as the building alarms went silent. Kek growled—his usual cold smirk plastered to his face—but kept his rifle sighted on me.

Several shots rang out.

Kek dropped to a knee, then immediately pushed himself back to his feet. I was in awe. The man couldn't be killed. He was like some kind of demonic Syrian superman.

No more had he regained his footing before he was met with another barrage of shots, this time forcing him to the floor. A black ball the size of a pea rolled slowly toward me along the marble floor. *Rubber bullets.*

Colonel Orabi and a squad of men gripping scratched riot shields, shotguns, and batons, approached from behind us. Pulling myself up, I watched Kek distrustfully until three of the colonel's men pushed him to the floor and wrapped his hands and feet with plastic zip ties.

"Colonel, I've never been so happy to see you," I said, extending my hand. "You're my hero."

He paused; then reluctantly shook it. "Flattery will not earn you forgiveness, Mr. Cogar. Had you done as I said and simply asked for my protection, you wouldn't have ended up in this mess."

Over my shoulder, I spotted Perry as he moved toward Kek's prone body like a child cautiously nearing the lion's den in a zoo.

"You're probably right. But it's hard to know who to trust sometimes," I said, remembering the words Aqiylah said when I first awoke after being drugged. "It's been a rough couple days."

"No one knows that more than me, Mr. Cogar. This may be my final act as an officer in this army." He glanced down at my bare feet—my once-khaki socks covered in filth—and shook his head disapprovingly, but didn't ask about my shoes.

"Well, I might be a little biased, but if this is your final act as an officer, I'm damn glad you chose to come help us."

Two soldiers, their riot masks raised, sprinted past bearing a man on a stretcher, one pinching an intravenous-fluid bag between his teeth—Sabi, hastily bandaged, bounced with each step the soldiers took. Exhausted from supporting her brother, Aqiylah seemed unable to keep up with the men carrying the stretcher,

"Will he survive?" she asked as she approached us, tears running down familiar paths on her cheeks.

The colonel beckoned one of his men over. "Sergeant Nagy, you were with Corporal Elzwary while he assessed the wounded man. Give us his likelihood of survival."

Nagy, distracted and uncomfortable with being put on the spot, spoke carefully. "Hard to say, sir. Elzwary managed to slow the bleeding, and assuming our men can get him through the crowds and to a medical facility in a timely fashion, I'd say he has a decent chance of survival."

With the sergeant's final words, Aqiylah slumped against my shoulder. I slipped an arm around her.

"You'll take us to him, right?" I asked.

"They'll take *her*, yes," the colonel said. "But you and I need to debrief."

"Come again?"

"Mr. Cogar, you seem to think that, because the country is crumbling around you, that entitles you to ignore the rules of a civilized society. You deliberately circumvented my guards at the hotel, falsely set off an emergency alarm at that same hotel during a time when law enforcement and medical aid was spread thin, initiated a high-speed chase through downtown Cairo that endangered the lives of dozens…."

"Initiated is the wrong word for that. I was an unwilling participant," I corrected. "And Perry set off the alarm at the hotel, not me."

"You then proceeded to level a museum filled with priceless and irreplaceable Islamic antiquities."

Looking around at the ravaged, bullet-ridden interior, I said, "Oh, this is the Museum of Islamic Art, isn't it? This was on my must-visit list."

"Well you did more than visit it, Mr. Cogar. You can congratulate yourself on that," the colonel said bitterly.

"Hey, I didn't shoot this place up. Sure, I may have broken a *few* things out of self-defense…." I said defiantly; then quickly realized that now was not the time to admit that. "But the fact is you've got psycho serial killers roaming the streets unchecked. We were just trying to survive. If anything, I think you and your countrymen owe me an apology."

Ignoring my retort, the colonel continued, "You have singlehandedly made my final days as a colonel in the Egyptian army the most difficult of my career."

I looked to my feet and sighed.

"Sorry about that."

Orabi eyed me curiously, and a thin smile formed on his lips.

"Well, consider yourself debriefed. On another note, you look just terrible. Perhaps you'd like to get cleaned up and join me for dinner?"

I paused as I tried to find a diplomatic way of turning him down. Before I could answer, Kek, carried by four of the colonel's men, floated by—snarling like a raccoon caught in a steel trap.

"I kill you, Cogar. I kill you, still."

"Sure you will," I reassured. Turning to the colonel and slapping a hand against his shoulder, I said, "You can't fault the guy's optimism, can you?"

"I cut your man parts and shove down throat; make you drown your own blood," Kek shouted.

"Yeah, I get it: very horrible, very terrifying. But you were going to do that before, too, remember? You've already played your trump card, slick. Enjoy your time in prison—I hear their softball team is the best in the league."

Kek chomped his teeth in my direction.

"Colonel, you might want to put a muzzle on this one. Don't want any of your boys contracting rabies."

As the colonel's men carried the mercenary away, Perry, following the procession, stopped and held out his hand to me.

"Cogar, in spite of everything, I think we did pretty damn good back there. I'm going to need a few weeks to decompress after all we've been through, but if I had to be in a jam like this, I'm actually glad it was with you. I think we make a pretty good team."

I stared at my feet as I mustered every ounce of humility I could. Perry looked at his outstretched hand uncomfortably. After a pause, I nodded my head and whispered, "I appreciate that, Perry." Reluctantly, I grabbed his hand and gave it a quick shake.

Smiling, relieved, Perry nodded to the colonel and walked toward the exit. Orabi, surprised at the earnestness with which Perry made his goodbye, said, "You two seem to have grown close in the last two days."

I shook my head and looked at the ceiling. "Yeah, as much as I hate to say this, I owe that asshole my life."

16

Friday of Departure

Sunlight flooded into the stark white hospital room, highlighting the dark gray wisps of errant cigarette smoke unwilling to leave through the open window.

"I heard Kek's dead," Sabi said before taking another deep drag on his cigarette. Aqiylah stood by the door, watching for nurses who might force him back into bed and scold us for smuggling him a pack of smokes.

"Good. Whatever that ugly bastard got was too good for him. Hell, just thinking about him gives me chills," I said, standing beside Sabi near the open window.

"Sounds like his time in prison wasn't pleasant."

"It seldom is," I said.

He looked at me quizzically before carefully blowing the smoke into the afternoon air. "I'd bet the Brotherhood had him killed to keep him from exposing any connection to their party."

"Well they've got the most to lose, now. Mubarak's all but out, and the people need a new leader."

"Leaders. Plural. They need a fucking parliament, not a different dictator."

"Right."

Sabi grunted and offered me his cigarette. I took it between my thumb and middle finger, drew in a deep breath, and tried to blow a smoke ring as I exhaled. It came out as an amorphous cloud, instead. Perching the coffin nail between my lips, I rubbed my injured wrist with my left hand.

"You still haven't had that looked at?"

"Naw. Can't write or type with a cast on."

"Seems unfair that I have to be stuck in this place and you get off without so much as an outpatient procedure."

"Life's unfair. Besides, you earned it by betraying us. If you hadn't gone running to the Brotherhood and led Kek back to us, you wouldn't have that hole in your chest. Karma's a frigid bitch, isn't she?"

"You know, Cogar, I still don't like you," Sabi said, plucking the cigarette from my lips.

"That's fine," I said, smiling.

"No, no it's not. *You* nearly got me killed. If *you* hadn't come to Egypt in the first place, none of this would have happened," he said, leaning in and lowering his voice. "If my sister didn't have such misguided affection for stupid men, I wouldn't be here."

"But then you wouldn't have that neat scar, either, would you?" I said, clapping my hand against the bandage wrapped around his middle. He gasped in pain. "Chicks dig scars."

"Grant, can I speak with you for a minute? In private," Aqiylah asked from the doorway.

I followed her into the hallway. She handed me Kek's video camera—the one I'd forgotten in her apartment.

"I thought you'd want this."

I laughed. "Thanks. I'd kinda forgotten about it. But you know, Aqiylah, I'm still going to have to fire you from your position as my translator. You haven't done anything but get me into trouble, and you haven't actually translated anything for me."

Ignoring my attempt at humor, she turned on her heel and checked to make sure no one was nearby. Running a finger over her ear, she tucked her hair back nervously.

"Hey. What is it?" I asked, touching her elbow. Her eyes glistened with tears. She stomped her foot and looked away as she wiped at them with the back of her hand. Finally, she whispered, "Grant, I love you. And before you say anything, I know you're not going to say you love me in return—I ruined any chance of you trusting me when I betrayed you."

"Like three times," I added.

She gave me a knowing, discouraged look. "I just want you to know that I'm sorry. I never meant to hurt you."

I bit my lower lip and stared into her eyes. She was stunning. A rare woman whose mind, body, and spirit were all things of extraordinary beauty. I took a deep breath.

"I don't hold any of that against you, Aqiylah, truly. I know you were just looking out for yourself and your brother, and I never felt like you wanted to see me hurt. But when you say that you love me, believe me, you don't."

"What gives you the right to say that? You may not love me in return, you're allowed that, but don't you dare tell me what I feel."

"Aqiylah, I respect you more than you know, and you are a gorgeous, intelligent woman worthy of only the best mankind has to offer. But you're young, too—really young. The last thing you need in your life is a relationship with a nomadic, alcoholic reporter who's ten years your elder."

"Oh, so this is you being chivalrous? Being too noble to allow me such a childish fantasy? I know who you are, Grant. Look at all we've been through together."

"But that's just it, Aqiylah. You're ignoring everything but what you're feeling at this instant. You won't think of me the same way in six months."

"Six months, six years, six decades. I'll always feel this way about you," she said, touching my hand. She wrapped her delicate fingers around my thumb, and though I wanted to return the touch, I ordered myself not to.

Aqiylah had seen more violence and had learned more painful lessons than most, but she was still, in so many ways, a child—just as any 18-year-old should be. It would be wrong of me to string her along or pretend that I could be the man she thought I was—it would be little more than a short-lived illusion. Though she may forever think of me as coldhearted and cruel for turning her away now, she would move on and be better for it. Frankly, I knew she could do better.

"If I call you in six months to remind you that I still feel the same way, will you reconsider?" she asked, the tears streaming unchecked down her cheeks.

I sighed and stepped forward. Cradling her head in my hands, I kissed her forehead gently. "Six months. Not a minute sooner."

******

Though it had been easy to forget with everything that had happened to us in the past few days, the uprising had finally achieved success. Shortly after I left the hospital, Mubarak gave a speech that many had anticipated would be his resignation. When the oppressive octogenarian finally came on, the entire city stood still. Even the cars and buses in the streets came to a halt as the country listened intently. The abrupt silence was jarring.

Then, he'd done exactly what I expected; he indignantly refused to resign. I flung my pen across the hotel room in disgust—I'd really been hoping that he would step down not only for the welfare of the country, but also for a tidy ending to my article. Instead, his vice president, Omar Suliman, followed with a speech that emptily promised change while reminding the people of Egypt that the foreign media shouldn't be trusted. The uproar that followed shook the city to its core. I spent the rest of the night listening to the familiar shouts and swelling roars of the crowds outside as the smoke from firebombs, burning tires, and fireworks fought its way inside the building's ventilation system.

Then, the next morning, just as I'd completed my story, the news came in that Mubarak had finally gotten the message and resigned, transferring the power of the country to the Supreme Council of the Armed Forces. Though this wasn't the monumental change most had hoped for—the army still controlled the country—it was an enormous step in the right direction. When I heard the news, I immediately tried to envision what Aqiylah's expression was at that moment, and briefly debated calling her up.

I didn't.

I convinced myself that she'd be too busy celebrating and I'd be too busy writing—rewriting—my article. Feeling a bit melancholy as I thought about her, I reminded myself that I had work to do. I decided I'd compromise between nostalgia and my job by typing up my article at the *kahwa* where Aqiylah and I had first sat down together. The Internet was back up, so I could finish my article and send it out without paying for postage or hiring some transient to sneak it out of the country for me.

During the time it took me to stroll down the street leading to the coffee shop, half a dozen strangers hugged me, overjoyed at the news of Mubarak's ouster. A group of soldiers, still in uniform, stopped and posed for a photo with me.

My smile looked forced.

Walking through the door to the shop, I glanced around for a minute, picked a corner table, and sat down. As the pleasingly familiar scent of fresh-ground coffee hung on the air, I stared at the table where Aqiylah and I had sat together a week before.

It had been a long while since I'd been so deeply conflicted about a girl. For a guy who made a habit of staying emotionally detached and keeping any relationships short-lived, I was struggling to suppress my feelings for Aqiylah. The problem, I knew, was that I was not only physically attracted to the girl, but sincerely valued her spirit and personality, too. Repeating to myself that if I actually cared about her, I'd leave her alone, I pulled out my laptop and began typing.

After an hour of mindlessly copying my previous drafts, I sipped at the lukewarm coffee in the bottom of my mug and typed out my article's last sentence. Before emailing it to Kailas, I pulled the memory card from

Kek's video camera and downloaded the files. The video would send a perfectly clear message to my mentor.

I earn my paycheck.

Bringing up the video player, I watched in grainy, low resolution as an unfamiliar scene played.

Three men in olive drab army uniforms—bruised, bloody, and narrowly clinging to consciousness as they stared at the camera—sat in a row atop a large decorative rug in the living room of a small house. Dust glittered in the afternoon sunlight as it streamed through the room's windows, the captive on the far right turning his swollen, bloodied face to the warmth as if to absorb it for the last time.

Kek's raspy voice narrated in Arabic as he moved from behind the camera to stand at the backs of his captives. The man was so brazen he didn't even bother to wear a *keffiyeh* or sunglasses to cover his features the way most terrorist types usually did. Grabbing a thick rope— already tied on one end with a noose—Kek slid it over the first captive's head. Tossing the free end of the rope over a ceiling joist, Kek planted a foot against the man's back and began raising him, pulling down on the rope, hand over hand. As the soldier's body danced, contorting helplessly as the noose crushed his windpipe, Kek tied off the line—leaving the man's feet inches from the floor—said a few more words, and then withdrew his knife and made a careful incision along the soldier's femoral artery. Blood immediately poured forth, staining his khaki pants and dripping down his leg. The captive grunted weakly, his thrashing dying down until he hung motionless, body swaying.

The second soldier, having watched the entire ordeal, mustered the strength to stand. Feet and hands bound, he hopped away from the camera. Kek, completely cool and still expressionless, used his free hand to slide a Makarov pistol from the small of his back. He fired twice in rapid succession. The second soldier collapsed, cried out in pain as his body writhed upon the floor, and died.

Amidst all this violence, the third soldier continued to stare at the window as if he hadn't heard or seen anything, the sunlight illuminating his face. Kek mumbled something final as he stepped toward the remaining soldier, knife in hand. Grabbing the man by the hair and jerking his head back, Kek grinned at the camera just before running the blade across the soldier's throat. The captive's eyes rolled back in his head as Kek began sawing at the flesh, working to decapitate his victim.

I gagged and looked away. I'd seen such ghastly acts before—spending most of my adult life in war zones made that a certainty. But I just never got used to it. Unlike some soldiers who simply turn that part of their humanity off—largely as a survival mechanism given their job—I still feel a crippling stab every time I witness someone having their life stolen from them. I guess it's because I still believe every being has a story, a culmination of irreplaceable experiences and emotions. When a life is ended prematurely, it feels as though the story has not only concluded too soon, but that all those singular experiences and emotions have been scattered like dust, relegated to the unadorned archives of history. And what resonates with me the most is that no death I've witnessed, not one, has resulted in a noticeable void, a pause, even the briefest recognition that a wealth of insight and knowledge and personality has been lost. The world continues on, humming along without the slightest interruption.

Maybe that's what drives me on as a reporter—the faint hope that those people's stories won't be forgotten, that someone somewhere will feel some twinge, even the smallest spark of pain, regret, or sadness, at their absence. And of course, I hope someone will do the same for me someday. I don't fear death—I can't in my line of work and get anything done—but I still battle with the notion that eventually I'll catch a bullet or shrapnel from an artillery shell and join the millions of others who left not one significant mark on the world beyond a smoking pile of entrails.

That said, I hoped that Kek enjoyed a fate worse than any he'd subjected others to during his miserable life. If I accomplished nothing else during my time here, I could rest a little easier each night knowing I'd had a hand in the bastard's death.

When I'd mustered the courage to look back at my computer screen, I felt relieved to find the scene had changed to the one featuring Perry and me in the garage. Exporting just that clip, I attached the file to the email and hit *send*. Closing my laptop, I sighed and leaned back in my chair.

I needed a fucking vacation.

In less than three months, I'd been in a car wreck, imprisoned and tortured repeatedly, drugged, beaten up, stabbed, shot, and nearly drowned. My role as an adventurer journalist was losing its shine. But as fatigued as I felt, I knew that a week back in Chicago would have me begging Kailas for a trip into some fresh new hellhole. Don't ask me why. I still don't know.

A buzzing vibration in my pocket told me Kailas had gotten my message.

"Hey Mom."

"Stow that shit, will you, Cogar? What the fuck am I looking at in this attached file?"

"You watched it yet? You should share that around the office—give me some street cred."

"Who's the one-eyed guy?"

"One very angry Syrian mercenary with an unusual attachment to the thought of killing yours truly."

"I guessed that last part. How'd you manage to piss him off?"

"Actually, I never really figured that out. I've slept with guys' wives and gotten less of a reaction than with this psycho. Must have reminded him of an old elementary school bully or something."

"Oh, holy shit. He actually stabbed you."

I laughed. "He was having a rough day."

"Jesus. Remind me to take out an extra large insurance policy on you when you get back."

"This isn't the worst treatment I've gotten, Kailas. If I keep managing to survive, I'd say the insurance idea is a bad investment."

"Your luck is going to run out one of these days, kid."

Kid? That's an unusually affectionate moniker coming from Kailas.

"Everything okay?"

"Yeah. But, well, holy shit, Cogar. I know you make a habit of getting into trouble during your exploits, but this is starting to get insane. Maybe we need to reassign you to something a little calmer stateside."

I smiled. Though seldom shown, Kailas did have a layer of humanity beneath his indifferent, hardened façade. He still viewed me as an adopted son of sorts, and it was actually a little heartwarming to know that, as much as he hated to admit it, my boss cared about my health and welfare.

"You've got a weird sense of humor, Kailas."

"I'm not kidding, you little fucker."

"When can I expect my plane ticket out of here?"

"Bought and paid for. Just run your company card through the machine at the airport. It should come up."

"You forbid me from carrying it, remember?"

"Oh that's right. Well, if you hadn't used it to buy a machine gun from an Israeli arms dealer, I would have let you keep it. What did you think was going to happen?"

"It wasn't just a machine gun; it was an Uzi—a fine piece of Israeli machinery. And I got it at an excellent price."

"What kind of arms dealer accepts credit cards, anyway?" the editor scoffed.

"He takes PayPal, too."

"Absurd. Anyway, I'll send you the card number. Give them that." Kailas paused; then said quietly, "Cogar, you should give some serious thought to hanging out back here for a few assignments."

"We can talk about it when I get back," I said dismissively.

"What's wrong with talking about it right now? Look, you're not a young man anymore, Cogar. You keep living this fast and dangerous lifestyle and it's going to catch up with you. You really want to die alone in some war-torn shithole without having made any lasting friends or started a family?"

"I've got you, don't I? You're like friends and family all wrapped up in one mean-spirited package.

Besides, there's no telling whether or not I've got kids out there somewhere. There've been a *lot* of women."

Ignoring my playful jab, he continued, "You just detest a domestic lifestyle because you've never lived it. Look at me; I get to go to my climate-controlled office every day, sleep in my own clean bed in my own clean home each night with my wife of 22 years, and have a comprehensive health and dental plan, and a 401k."

"Sounds like absolute hell. And what's a four oh one kay?" I asked, slowly pronouncing each number.

"Funny. But seriously, Cogar, I've got it easy, and you could too. The biggest concern in my life is a toss up between making sure my car starts during the winter and Julie doesn't fall for a high school dropout. Doesn't that sound a little more appealing than being strung up and stabbed?"

"How old is she now? It's been so long since I've seen any of the kids."

"Just turned 16."

"Hard for me to picture her as a grown woman," I said, leaning back in my chair and rubbing the stubble on my chin.

"Imagine how hard it is for me."

I listened to the static airwaves, neither of us speaking for a few seconds. He continued, "Do I occasionally wish I could travel the world like you? Sure. Do I admire your courage and devil-may-care attitude? Yeah, sometimes I do. But it's unsustainable. You keep running at this pace, you're going to burn out. You'll fall off the map, and I'll end up hearing rumors that you shaved your head and ran off to join some Buddhist monastery in Tibet."

"Really? I always fancied myself joining the French Foreign Legion or becoming one of those military contractors back in the Stan."

"You think those skull stompers would take you? You even whisper the word 'journalist' in their presence and they'd rip your limbs off. Besides, you've said it yourself; you don't have the stomach for killing. You'd be a terrible mercenary."

"Ah, but my bullet-dodging skills are known worldwide. I'm surprised they haven't come knocking with a job offer yet."

Kailas didn't answer. It'd been years since I'd heard him this solemn, and I began to wonder what had brought about the drastic change in his demeanor.

Sighing, I said quietly, "Kailas, I've been doing this non-stop for a decade, and sure, it's cost me more than my fair share of blood in the process and given me a few prematurely gray hairs. But if I haven't grown tired of it yet, I doubt I ever will. It's not that I can't understand how your cozy editor's position wouldn't appeal to some people, but it's just not me."

"I wasn't offering you my position, you arrogant little shit."

"That's fine; I don't want it. Go home, kiss Dannielle, give the kids a hug for me, and let me do my thing. I'll come in and say hi when I get back stateside. When you give me my paycheck, I'll even take you out for a beer. We can talk shop."

"Alright, Cogar," Kailas said wearily. "I'm off to the liquor store."

I checked the time and did the math in my head. "It's only 11 o' clock over there."

"It is. Means I'm an hour overdue for a drink. Didn't factor in speaking to you, so I might as well make it a double."

"Funny."

"Oh, and I haven't had a chance to get all the way through your article yet. No doubt that'll drive me to finish the bottle."

"You're fucking hilarious, Kailas."

"If it turns out to be decent, I might even bump that riveting piece I got in from Warren about Estonia's adoption of the Euro for the front page."

"Most of our readers couldn't point out Estonia on a map."

"True. Speaking of which, I have noticed you're getting a little lofty in your writing style. Keep in mind that most of our readers have the vocabulary and maturity of a second grader. You're not writing for the *Times*, here."

Kailas's mention of Perry's publication caused me to envision my rival walking through the front doors of the New York Times Building wearing one of his tailored Brooks Brothers suits, silk tie, and a smile that'd have women fawning over him as though he were a cardboard box filled with puppies. As much as it killed me to say it, I had begun to reconsider my grudge against Perry. Though I hadn't forgotten all the rapacious, mean-spirited things he'd done to me in the past, it occurred to me as I lay in bed the night before that I'd become so obsessed with the notion of besting my rival that I'd ignored my intuition and nearly gotten myself killed. From that realization came another—if I'd really wanted Perry's job, the one I thought I deserved, I knew enough people in the industry where I could probably get an interview at the *Times*. The problem was, I didn't want Perry's job. I just wanted him *not* to have it. Was that juvenile? Probably. I mean, I understood why I felt the way I did; anyone who had been ripped-off as overtly as I had would want some kind of karmic justice dealt. And because the article I'd written had earned Perry a Livingston Award and his position at the Times, I felt as though the accolade and all that had followed belonged to me. But did going out of my way to humiliate and undermine him for the rest of my days make us even? Did it even make sense, practically speaking? No. It was beginning to become a distraction that was doing me more harm than good. Besides, he *had* saved my life back at the Museum of Islamic Art. Had he done what I would have and let Kek's thug put a rifle round through my dome, I wouldn't be able to continue hating him because I'd be resoundingly defunct. That wasn't something I took lightly. I've always subscribed to the notion of life debt—where the person who's been saved by another is indebted to his savior until he returns the favor. I wasn't pleased that I owed Perry my life, but I had no doubt that there would come a time when our paths would cross again and an opportunity to pay him back would present itself.

"Hey, before I let you go," I continued as Kailas mumbled something along the lines of 'I don't care what her reasoning is, I'm not running that fucking novel-length article in my newspaper' to his assistant, "if you're still at the office, would you mind checking to see if I got any mail from Jennifer Sedgewick? She promised to get me some contractual paperwork for freelance work."

"Wait, first of all, who the fuck do you think you are, having other publications send their shit here? You don't even have a desk here, and you've got a perfectly functional mailbox at home. Second, you mean *the* Jennifer Sedgewick? The magazine publisher? What the hell would she want with…oh no way. You slept with her, didn't you?"

"One could make the argument that *she* slept with *me*. But yes. Yes, I did. I call it 'networking'." I grinned, recalling the night we'd spent together. She'd been a wildcat. Even if nothing came of the job opportunity, it'd been worth it.

"You're possibly the most shameless, depraved man I know."

"Flatterer."

Kailas groaned. "Look, I've got to go. Some of us have work to do—not that you'd know anything about that."

"Don't lie to me, Kailas. You run a newspaper—your readers hate you and only subscribe for the coupons and to give them something new to criticize. You could run nothing but repeats of op-ed columns and not lose a single subscriber," I said, flicking a crumb from the tabletop.

"I'm fine with that as long as they keep writing us checks and the ad revenue keeps coming in."

"Glad you've got your priorities straight."

"Damn right. Someday you will too. Enjoy your last night in Cairo, Cogar."

"I'll try, thanks. Have a good one, Kailas."

Just after ending the call, my phone emitted a loud *badink*. I began scanning Aqiylah's text message, my heart racing despite my attempt to remain indifferent. It read, "It's a beautiful night, meet me on the roof of your hotel and watch the sunset with me."

I began punching buttons in reply, but stopped and returned it to my pocket. It was difficult to say whether Aqiylah had accepted my terms—understanding that I'd be leaving—and was only wanting to say goodbye, or if she was entertaining some naïve obsession with me that she couldn't turn off. In either case, sitting with her on a rooftop, alone, watching the setting sun on one of the nation's most historic days was a surefire way for me to end up doing something I'd regret. Willpower, especially when it comes to life's more carnal pleasures, is not something I possess an abundance of. If you look on my resume under skills and qualifications, debauchery and lechery are towards the top.

"Excuse me, sir. We're going to close a little early, if you don't mind," said the store proprietor.

Looking around, I realized I was the only customer.

"I'm sorry. Of course—it's too beautiful a day to be working, anyway."

He grinned and nodded. Tossing my laptop in my bag and slinging the strap over my shoulder, I stepped out onto the sidewalk.

Despite my better judgment, I wanted to go see Aqiylah once more before I left. I would just have to maintain control over myself, which, even as I stood there waiting for a break in traffic, struck me as a ridiculous notion. I was voluntarily putting myself into a situation where I'd be alone with a supple-bodied 18-year-old infatuated with me. It didn't take a psychic to know how that would play out. What I needed to do—which would be better for both of us—was make a beeline for the airport and catch the first flight back to the States, putting the memory of Aqiylah and this country behind me. But clearly the angel on my shoulder wasn't shouting loudly enough to be heard above my thoughts of an empty hotel room—paid up through the night on the colonel's dime— and Aqiylah's lean, sun-kissed body, because back to my hotel I went.

Entering the empty lobby, I locked my attention on the door leading to the stairway and stepped toward it hurriedly. Maybe that's why I completely missed seeing her.

Shoved headlong through the door into the empty stairwell, I wheeled around—fists up—to find Sally Parker blocking the door, chewing her lip as she eyed me eagerly.

"Oh, for the love of God, could we please not do this again?" Striving to recall my teenage years and how I'd let girls down easy back then, I said, "You're a nice girl and all, and I'd really like to sit down and talk about this sometime. Maybe grab a cup of coffee. But now really doesn't work for me."

"You didn't have time for me before, either. Now you're going to make time," she said seductively as she licked her lips.

"Lady, I don't know what is going on in that crazy, bipolar brain of yours, but you need to get over this notion of you and me enjoying each other's company—in a biblical sense or otherwise."

"How are you going to stop me?" she asked not so much as a challenge, but out of curiosity.

"I was kinda hoping that telling you I'm not interested would suffice."

"But you'd get physical with me if you had to, right?"

"I was really hoping it wouldn't come to that."

"But you would?" she asked as she thumbed open the topmost buttons on her blouse.

"Yeah, I guess," I stuttered as I stared at her bosomy figure.

"You promise?" she asked, rushing towards me and gripping the back of my neck with both hands.

"Sally, stop."

"Oh come on, don't be afraid of me," she whispered in my ear, her warm breath tickling me as she slid her body against mine.

I won't lie, at that moment—already excited by what awaited me on the rooftop—I gave some serious thought to capitulating and appeasing Sally's voracious sexual appetite with a few good thrusts before moving on with my day. But I wasn't a completely wanton whore, and knowing that Aqiylah was waiting for me nearby helped to ease any urges I might otherwise delight in quenching with Sally. But just because I'd made up my mind to stay the course didn't mean she was going to let me leave. I envisioned arriving on the rooftop with Sally firmly affixed to my leg like some lascivious leech.

In an attempt to distract her from her insistent advances, I asked, "So, I have to ask, what brought about this change in perspective? Every time we've been near one another, you've made it perfectly clear that you hate the very fiber of my being."

"They say opposites attract. Just because I hate everything you say and stand for doesn't mean I don't find you irresistibly sexy." She slid my belt open and began unzipping my pants.

Realizing that Sally had no interest in talking and would proceed with her eager pursuit regardless of how much I tried to dissuade her, I formulated a quick plan.

Behind her, a broom hung suspended from a steel hook. Knocking it to the floor, I wrapped my arms around Sally, pinning her against the wall with my body, and whispered in my deepest baritone, "Tell me how much you hate me."

She squealed with pleasure as I slipped my hands down her legs and lifted her to my waist, her chest at my eye level.

"You're so strong," she moaned.

Gently slipping her belt over the steel hook in the wall, I pulled away and left her swinging, her feet six inches from the floor. "Thanks," I said, dusting my hands and admiring my handiwork. "I don't get to the gym as much as I'd like, but I still try."

"Cogar, what are you doing?" she asked, the seduction vanishing from her voice, her familiar angry growl taking its place.

"Oh, I just remembered I've got somewhere else I've got to be. I'll come back when you've had a little time to cool off."

"Cogar, you ungrateful, conceited, self-centered bastard, get back here!"

"You know, when I said to tell me all the ways you hate me, I didn't actually mean it. I'd prefer if you kept those to yourself. I have a fragile ego."

"You're an arrogant, impotent, gutless man-slut, Cogar."

"Hey now; that's just slanderous. I'm not impotent."

Turning away from my irate would-be lover—chuckling to myself as she cursed under her breath and noisily tried to disentangle herself from her perch on the wall—I climbed the stairwell two stairs at a time until I reached the rooftop. Swinging open the door, I felt my heart drop in my chest as though someone had swung a sledgehammer atop it.

Rather than finding Aqiylah standing seductively before the brilliant sunset wearing nothing but a negligee and a look of barely-constrained anticipation, I found her with a knife to her throat—Kek gripping the blade with that familiar sick, hollow grimace upon his face.

17

Purposeless Annihilation

"I'm not gonna lie, I was really hoping you'd fallen on a shiv in prison," I mumbled as adrenaline pulsed through my system, my body temperature rising as I anticipated a fight. "You know, Kek, you've really been the icing on the cake of this profoundly shitty assignment. I didn't get to unearth any antiquities or ride a camel, all because I've been too busy trying to keep you from killing me."

"I'm so sorry, Grant," Aqiylah whimpered. "He made me send that message."

"I know. It's okay, Aqiylah. We're going to be fine," I said as reassuringly as I could, sliding my suit jacket off and rolling my shirtsleeves to my elbows.

"I tell you, I kill you still. You think you escape Egypt before I escape prison? No," Kek said, snaking the blade closer to Aqiylah's trachea.

"Let her go, and you and I can settle this. It's a personal dispute between you and me. Not her."

I'd seen only one hostage situation that had ended well, and it had been swiftly and neatly resolved by a Marine squad designated marksman and one carefully placed round from his .300 Winchester Magnum at about 300 meters. Clearly, I wasn't in a position to employ such a convincing negotiating tool. That left me with only one viable option: To talk him down. With a zealot like Kek—whose mastery of the English language narrowly surpassed that of the orangutans at the Giza Zoo—that was about as likely as the Chicago Cubs winning a World Series.

Realizing this dilemma, Aqiylah suddenly cried, "Grant, run!" as she ducked Kek's blade and brought an elbow against his chest. Instinctively, his free hand lashed out and struck her beneath the chin. Stumbling backwards, I could only watch in horror as she tripped over the building's edge and disappeared from view.

I leapt toward her in an attempt to stop her fall, but was too late. She was gone.

From the corner of my eye I saw Kek make a similar effort. We both stared at the building's edge, stunned.

Two things crossed my mind simultaneously: The first was why Kek hadn't shot Aqiylah in the museum—insane as he was, the bastard seemed to draw the line at killing women. He clearly hadn't intended to send her off the rooftop, and the shocked expression plastered to his jaundiced face affirmed it.

The second was that I'd failed Aqiylah. The girl had loved me and I'd been helpless to save her. My eyes shifted away from the building's edge as I felt a bloodlust growing in my chest with such ferocity I thought I might vomit. My hands shook as they tightened into fists.

Thinking back to Aqiylah's sweet face, I realized I didn't just want to kill this bastard to avenge her; I wanted him to suffer for what he'd done. The murderer before me was the manifestation of all things wrong with the world— the cause of every destroyed village, every genocide, every execution and assassination I'd ever bore witness to and was helpless to stop. He represented purposeless annihilation, and I owed it to Aqiylah to wipe his worthless being from existence.

"Her soul rests with Allah now," Kek said, his voice wavering as he tossed his blade from one hand to another. "Your soul rest with Allah soon."

"Yeah? Well Allah called and said you sent the wrong person. He's waiting for you, asshole, and I'm gonna give you to him."

I wrapped my jacket loosely around my left arm. The thin fabric wouldn't stop Kek's blade, but it might keep the wounds shallow enough for me to continue the fight, so long as I managed to block his strikes. Rushing forward, I narrowly dodged as Kek swung his knife toward my neck—a lightning fast lunge, the knife blade little more than a glitter of light. Swinging a hard right, I felt my knuckles connect with his jaw. An instant reminder of my injuries, pain bolted up my arm into my neck. Kek, quick to sense weakness, grinned, spat, and shifted his attack to my right side—sweeping the blade at my chest, then following through with a backhanded strike from his left hand.

The fucker's knuckles felt like stone.

Reeling, I felt the warmth of fresh blood flow from my split lip. *Focus on the blade, Cogar. You can take a beating all day from this guy, but he'll bleed you dry if he connects with that toad sticker.*

I swung my cloth-covered arm at the Syrian's temple, leaving my chest exposed. With a front thrust kick, he sent me stumbling backward. A bundle of Ethernet cables strapped to the rooftop caught my ankle, and I pitched over—falling hard to the concrete.

"I tell you," he said, stepping toward me deliberately, rubbing his fingers against his knife blade's sides, "game never escapes hunter." Moving the knife to his eye patch, he slipped the steel beneath the fabric and lifted it slowly to reveal a mutilated, umbrageous chasm so horribly disfigured I recoiled in disgust. His eyeball alone hadn't been excised from the skull: instead, the entire socket had been crushed and torn—slivers of ruptured bone still raw and exposed through the sickly pink tissue spanning from the man's brow to his cheek. That empty void stared back at me as the mercenary whispered, "Libya, mortar bomb esplode nearby. World go dark. One hour, I wake. Friends, dead. Brother, dead." He paused, the slightest glimmer of human emotion wavering in his voice. "Bomb take Kek's eye. But I not dead. I find mortar men, take knife—" he made a series of quick stabbing and slashing motions to illustrate his story.

Feeling a thin layer of dusty sand beneath my hand, I quietly swept a handful into my palm.

"I kill all. You, you not mortar men," his voice rose in volume as anger overcame him. "You not soldier. Not gun. Not bomb. Weak. But you run fast as rabbit. So I hunt you like rabbit. Today, I taste your flesh."

Dropping toward me suddenly, Kek lunged—his knife pointed at my chest. Slinging my handful of sand into his face as I rolled to my side, the blade struck the concrete roof and snapped beneath Kek's body weight.

Undeterred, the Syrian dove at me again, the jagged, broken steel aimed at my throat. Rolling onto my shoulders, I planted both my feet against his chest and, using his momentum, launched him over my head. I felt the mercenary's bony fingers wrap themselves in my shirt as he pitched over the building's threshold, and was quickly dragged toward my attacker and the precipice that promised certain death for both of us. Gripping the roof's edge with both hands, I struggled to stay atop the building as Kek swung below—still trying to stab me with his free hand. Daring a glance over my shoulder, I was met with a stunning view of the rolling river water of the Nile. A familiar terror seized my insides like a steel trap.

****

Chicago, Illinois, August 1995

"Jump!" cried the other teens crowding behind me on the narrow Algonquin Road Bridge. Though Salt Creek held enough water to be considered a river, it moved at a trickling pace for most of the year. I clung to the concrete abutment and stared at the swirling eddies of opaque water below. It was a short plunge: The water was no more than ten feet deep, and it couldn't be more than fifty feet from either shoreline. I briefly imagined myself slipping into the water and

walking along the sandy bottom toward the bank. No one would know that I didn't have a clue how to swim. This wasn't crossing the English Channel—it was a childishly simple task, and surely one I could succeed at as long as I stay focused.

"Come on, just jump already."

"Anyone check the depth? I don't want to break my neck when I go in," I said.

"It's plenty deep. We've been swimming here for years. Just jump."

The summer sun made my pale skin tingle as a single bead of sweat slipped from my forehead to my ear and down my neck. The algal smell of the water blended with the smoke from a cigarette one of the kids had stolen from his father and was now passing around.

"Alright, here I go," I said, trying to sound as cool as possible, though I noticed a slight quiver in my voice. Forcing my fingers from their grip on the concrete, I heaved myself out over the water as though some demon within me, at odds with my better senses, had shoved me off. I fell through the air, my heart racing as I wrapped my knees to my chest and prepared to hit the water's surface.

Sploosh.

I began paddling for the surface before the cool sensation of the water even registered in my mind. Kicking wildly, I broke through to the sunshine and gasped, a smile finding my lips as I realized I'd survived; this swimming thing wasn't so hard. See, Cogar? You just had to put your mind to it.

Hearing my friends shouting at me, I laughed and managed a wave, cementing my uncaring, cool-guy persona in their eyes, I was sure. But their shouts continued as I paddled, their voices suddenly taking on meaning.

"Grant, swim for shore! The current, Grant—swim for the bank!"

Looking confusedly about, I felt a fresh new panic squeeze my chest as I found myself gaining momentum, pulled away from the bridge and dragged downriver. As panic set in, my method for staying afloat shifted to madly clawing and thrashing; I quickly exhausted myself trying, unsuccessfully, to navigate to the shore. Water splashed at the corners of my mouth and flooded up my nostrils as I struggled for breath. As I went under, my eyes caught the glittering, crystalline rays of sunshine as they danced upon the surface, and I knew with absolute certainty that this would be my last moment alive.

****

That moment *hadn't* been my last. Within seconds of going under, my feet scraped along a sand bar, and I'd managed to drag myself to shore, drinking deeply at the fresh air as I came to the surface and swearing off swimming forever. Water and I have not, and likely never will, get along. I'd love to make my peace with the stuff, but whenever I hop in anything deeper than a bathtub, it tries to drown me. Though I might survive the multi-story drop from my hotel's rooftop, I was pretty damn sure I wouldn't overcome the depths of the river below.

"Get off me, Syrian Cyclops," I said through gritted teeth. I was losing my grip, and if something didn't happen quickly, my strength would give out and we'd both be killed.

Better a controlled fall than one I'm unprepared for.

Struggling to overcome my dread, my eyes wide and breathing rapid, I abandoned my handhold, letting myself tumble over the edge—my legs coming up and over my head. Reaching out, I narrowly snagged a hand on the building's ledge a few feet below, my body swinging above the abyss. The short drop forced Kek to adjust his hold from my shirt to a tenuous one on my pant leg, his fingers sliding gradually down my calf. Though I struggled to keep my grip, I consciously looked down at Kek.

He just stared at me, the same empty, inhuman, apathetic glare he always wore. No pleading for his life, no panic-lined features—he was stone.

And he dropped like one.

Planting the heel of my shoe against his forehead, I gave a mighty shove. No cry escaped his lips as he plunged through the air, his body falling away cleanly— legs and arms held outright. And he held that stare until his body came to an abrupt halt, his spine crushed as it wrapped around the cannon of an abandoned Ramses battle tank parked below.

"I guess the water wasn't as close as I thought." Looking back at my straining, bloodless fingers as they slowly gave to my body weight, I took a deep breath, thinking of Aqiylah once more as I prepared to abandon myself to a similar fate.

Oddly, I felt at peace with the world, as though this had always been the plan. An Egyptian sunset warmed my back, the vermillion-hued rays glittering on the Nile's softly lapping waves. I'd had a good run, lived a life filled to the breaking point with adventure and excitement, and if I had to go, I would want it to end like this. Kailas would understand. Closing my eyes, I embraced the sensation of falling away, freefalling toward the sandy earth below.

But before I'd dropped a foot, strong fingers wrapped around my wrist, halting my descent. Aqiylah's face peeked over the building's top, her slim arms straining to lift me up.

"Come on, Grant. Help me."

"Aqiylah? You're okay," I said, relief and a revitalized energy flooding through my veins. With a newfound grip and Aqiylah's body weight lifting me, I scrambled up the building's face and quickly wrapped her in my arms, kissing her neck, lips, and brow. "I thought he'd killed you."

"He nearly killed both of us," she said between kisses. "I thought I'd led you to your death. Grant, I'm so sorry for everything. Please forgive me."

I smiled, my nose touching hers as I admired the sunset's rays in her eyes; then ran my fingers through her hair as I brought my lips tightly to hers.

18

A New Day

"Things seem quieter now," I said, looking out over the city from the hotel's rooftop. Aqiylah and I sat together on an aluminum air duct, her hand in mine. Though the streets still glowed with the dying embers of burning tires and trash, the honking car horns and the loud cheers and trills of the protesters had faded to a distant throb. The people had finished the day's fight and celebration of victory, retiring now to their homes and awaiting whatever the next day would bring.

Aqiylah tilted her head and wiped away a tear as it slipped from her eye. I couldn't tell if she was crying with joy at the success of her people or with sadness at the thought of me leaving the next day. Though conceited, part of me hoped it was the latter.

"You did it, Aqiylah," I said, rubbing my thumb against the top of her hand.

"We're not there yet. But I'm happier today than I've been in my entire life." Turning to look at me, her eyes glittering with tears, she continued, "And, at the same time, more unhappy than I've ever been."

From the street, a soft, voiceless song echoed from a car radio. Standing, I slipped a hand around Aqiylah's lithe waist—pulling her against me softly. As though I had just broken down a thin, transparent wall that had stood between us, she fell into my embrace, wrapping her arms around my neck and nuzzling my ear.

"Six months," she whispered. "Right? Just six more months."

A breeze swept through our hair as the sun made its final descent into the horizon, and we danced, her head on my shoulder.

"You know, Aqiylah," I said wistfully, her dark hair brushing against my lips. "I'm leaving tomorrow, and I never did get that camel ride."

Arab Spring Leads to Mubarak's Fall

By Grant Cogar

CAIRO – The people of Egypt may be the most enduring of any in the world. After years of being subjugated by an oppressive dictator— suffering poverty, a police force known for brutality and corruption, and a fraudulent voting system—they've risen up in one of the largest protests the country has ever seen, spurred on by the successful riots in Tunisia weeks before. In return, they've been mercilessly sprayed with fire hoses, fired upon with rubber bullets, and beaten by camel-mounted thugs on President Hosni Mubarak's payroll. Yet they persist.

Today, their sacrifices proved worthwhile: After thirty years of power, the Egyptian people have finally ousted Mubarak from power. Though control of the country has shifted to the Supreme Council of the Armed Forces for the moment, hopes remain high that a democratic government emphasizing personal freedoms will soon replace the currently military-dominated one.

This could only have been achieved through the resolve of Egyptians like Ahmed Ghoneim, a professor at Sinai University and political activist. Marching toward Tahrir Square, everything about his body language clearly showed he was unafraid of the threat of imprisonment or death. "Mubarak has always proudly exercised his power while hiding behind his army," he said. "But now, with the entire nation coming down upon him and his soldiers leaving his side for our cause, we have proven to him and to the world that now is the time for a new Egypt."

Mubarak's soldiers, though by and large still loyal to their uniform, recognized their predicament and the overwhelming extent of the uprising. When asked about the severity of the protests, Colonel Saif al-Orabi of the Jihaz Amn ad-Daoula—the State Security Investigations

Service—said with fatigue lining his voice, "Looting has become rampant. Prisons have been burned down and inmates scattered to the wind, the police withdrawn from the streets and our soldiers brought in."

For Aqiylah Ibrahim, a young woman caught up in the turmoil of the rebellion and a reluctant member of the Muslim Brotherhood—one of the largest political opposition organizations vying for control of Egypt, and Islamic fundaments—this conflict represents a chance for fair, democratic elections, though at the cost of continued suppression of women's rights. "This government has been broken for years, and to fix it, to have our voices heard without fear of soldiers kicking in our doors in the night, without our people being beaten and interrogated, we need to ally ourselves with anyone who might help us. Right now, the Muslim Brotherhood is the best chance we've got to oust the president and finally have democratic elections."

Perhaps that's the reason this conflict has been so difficult for the government to control or for outsiders to fully understand. So many different players want such a diverse range of eventualities to result from it. But one thing remains constant among all of those involved—the driving desire for change and peace.

Even with so many uncertainties for the future of Egypt, news of the president's resignation and incarceration symbolizes a hard won success. Tears of exhausted joy cover most faces, falling atop streets still wet with gasoline and blood. A tangible sense of relief hangs on the air—shared by soldiers and citizens alike—the battle-weary people of Egypt able to rest for the moment.

If these protests stand out in the annals of history, it will be the people's inspirationally unwavering resistance to adversity that makes it so.

Cogar will return in *Cogar's Crusade*.

For more of Nate Granzow's work, visit nategranzow.com.

If you enjoyed *Cogar's Revolt*, be sure to read the first book in the Cogar Adventure series, *Cogar's Despair*.

Mounting an unprovoked artillery attack on the South Korean island of Yeonpyeong, North Korea has pushed international relations to the breaking point. With the civilian death toll mounting by the minute, the world stands by with bated breath, awaiting the coming of a second Korean War. The Chicago Herald prepares to send their best reporter to cover this desperate event as it spirals out of control. Only, their best also happens to be the most crass, alcoholic, and prodigious womanizer the journalism world has ever seen. His name is Grant Cogar.

A man so familiar with dodging shrapnel and sleeping in foxholes that it feels like sport, Cogar readily agrees to travel to Seoul—a vacation opportunity, as he sees it. But upon arrival, he quickly finds that the story he was meant to uncover has nothing to do with politics or war, but is instead hidden in the faint white powder beneath an old friend's nose.

Quietly pursuing a network of violent drug smugglers into downtown Shanghai, China, Cogar will need to use every ounce of his cunning and cleverness to outwit these hardened criminals, keep his friend and himself alive, and come away with an article his readers want to cut out and tape to their refrigerators.

COGAR'S REVOLT

For another award-winning thriller set in Egypt, check out Steven Hildreth Jr.'s premier novel, *The First Bayonet*.

2006, Cairo. Egyptian/American citizen Zaina Anwar has been imprisoned by the Mubarak government for subversion. Her cousin, a member of Egypt's elite Unit 777, reaches out to former Delta Force operator Ben Williams with a plea--break his cousin out of prison and ferry both of them to political asylum in the US.

What starts off as a simple rescue operation explodes into an international incident. Trapped in the city and hung out to dry, Williams must use his wits to stay one step ahead of the Egyptian government and escort Zaina and her cousin to safety.

NATE GRANZOW

Though young compared to many accomplished authors, Nate Granzow's experience with the written word surpasses his years. A Drake University graduate, he holds dual degrees in English writing and magazine journalism. His work has been showcased in over 10 professional publications and he currently works as an editor for a major woodworking magazine. An outdoorsman and adventurer, his writing strikes at the thrill-seeker in all of us.

Made in the USA
Charleston, SC
25 November 2015